Murder In Key West 9

Edited by
Shirrel Rhoades

ABSOLUTELY AMAZING eBOOKS

Habent Sua Fata Libelli

ABSOLUTELY AMAZING eBOOKS

Manhanset House
Shelter Island Hts., New York 11965-0342

bricktower@aol.com • tech@absolutelyamazingebooks.com
• absolutelyamazingebooks.com

Library of Congress Cataloging-in-Publication Data
Rhoades, Shirrel, editor
Murder In Key West 9
p. cm.

1. Fiction / Thrillers / Suspense. 2. Fiction / Mystery & Detective /
Collections & Anthologies. 3. Fiction / Thrillers / Crime. Fiction, I. Title.
ISBN: 978-1-955036-45-0, Trade Paper

March 2023

Murder In Key West 9

Murder and Mayhem In Paradise

Edited by
Shirrel Rhoades

The pen is mightier than the sword, they say. But what about weapons ranging from flare guns to spear guns to a coconut? You'll find them all in this murderous anthology.

Here's to those who plot such murders –
mystery writers!

Introduction

About The Authors

Introduction
To Mayhem

As the title implies, this is the ninth year of collecting short mysteries about crime in Key West. Those who live here know that murder and such is very rare. Most of it takes place on the pages of novels by writers like Bill Craig, Michael Haskins, Tom Dorsey, and Tom Corcoran.

But the island – the southernmost point in the continental United States – is a setting that's perfect for fictional shoot-outs and stabbings, drownings and strangulations. Maybe it's the natural contrast between dark deeds and eye-dazzling scenery, a picture-postcard world that has in real life seen pirates and plunderers, drug smugglers and CIA operations.

This annual series celebrates those writers who focus on the mystery genre – in particular (as the subtitle suggests) murder and mayhem in Paradise.

-Shirrel Rhoades
Key West

1. Coconut Kill

Bill Craig

Key West is a place where the strange and absurd become commonplace, so it was no surprise really when Paloma Green hired us to investigate the mysterious death of her cousin Mal. By us, I mean my cousin Rick Marlow and myself. The name is Greg and I have been handling the investigations while Rick is recovering from not only being shot by Russian mobsters, but having to have the rest of a lung removed as well because of the damage the bullets had done.

Anyway, Mal had been found dead on Caroline Street near the Key West Cemetery. Normally, private investigators tend to steer away from active murder investigations, but Paloma was a friend, so I figured it wouldn't hurt to dig in around the edges as long as I didn't interfere with the police investigation. I really shouldn't call it an active murder case, because they were calling it a suspicious death investigation.

The body had already been taken away by the time I got to the scene of the crime, but the blood was still in place on the sidewalk. According to Paloma, it looked like someone had bludgeoned Mal from behind.

I took a look around and didn't see anything unusual of out of place, other than palm leaves and a couple of coconuts that had been blown out of the trees by the storm the night before. It had been a violent one with 40 mile an hour wind gusts. Because of the storm not a lot of folks had been out on the streets. Even the folks of Key Weird knew not to tempt fate if it could be avoided. Except for Mal Green. I didn't know what had brought him out in the night, but I hoped that it had been worth it for him, given that he was now dead.

His body had been found by a patrol officer a couple of hours after the storm had finally passed. After seeing all I could at the scene of his death, I headed for the Key West Police Station. I wanted to see if Chief Gutierrez and his people had come up with anything yet. I didn't have the same rapport with the Chief that Rick had, but then Rick had known the guy longer and the Chief and I had gotten off to a bit of a rocky start when I had tracked down the Bratva gangsters that were responsible for Rick being shot and his client/girlfriend being killed before he and his people did. Apparently, it made him look bad.

The sun was up and the day was getting hotter and more humid by the minute. Sweat had already plastered the light cotton aloha shirt to my back. I was glad for the khaki-colored cargo shorts I had put on this morning. My Ruger SR40 Compact was snugged in the right front pocket inside its pocket holster. I never left the office without it. I had an identical spare hidden away on my recently replaced boat *The Wayfarer.*

I had bought it with the insurance settlement I got after my last boat had been blown up in the Key West Bight. I lived aboard because dock space was cheaper than renting an apartment. There were plenty of other folks that lived aboard so it was like living in a small neighborhood where everybody looked out for each other.

Once I reached the front desk, I asked to see the Chief and checked my gun with the desk sergeant. Jamie Gutierrez had his office on the second floor. Today he was wearing a white shirt, silver-colored tie and grey linen pants. He frowned when he looked up at me. I couldn't help but think he looked like the guy that had played Captain Castillo on the old TV series Miami Vice.

"What have I done to deserve you so early in the morning?" he asked.

"I knew I should have brought a *Café Con Leche* and some donuts."

"Ha ha. Seriously Greg, why are you here?"

"Paloma Green asked me to look into Mal's death. Any idea what caused it yet?" I asked as I dropped into the chair on the opposite side of his desk.

"Preliminary cause is blunt force trauma to the back of his head. Beyond that, we are still investigating it as a suspicious death," he told me.

"Homicide?"

"We don't know yet. So, I guess you can look into it," the Chief told me. I thanked him and then got out of there before he changed his mind. It was time to talk to Paloma again and see if she had any new ideas.

Paloma Green was on the young side of thirty with shoulder-length brown hair, coffee colored skin and intense blue eyes. She was wearing a yellow tube top that offer a nice view of her assets. Dark blue booty shorts covered the bottom and flip-flops completed her ensemble. She looked at me expectantly as she opened the door in answer to my knock. "Marlow, have you found something already?" she asked in a sultry voice that could entrance any man who heard it.

"Not yet. The police are calling it a suspicious death, but not a homicide. At least not yet. Have you thought of anybody that might want to hurt Mal?" I asked, stepping inside. Paloma remained quiet as she led me into the small living room of her house.

"Can I get you something to drink? Water, coffee, sweet tea?" she asked.

"No thanks. What about my question?"

"Everybody liked Mal. You know how he was, always the life of the party and a peacemaker when there was trouble," Paloma shrugged. She was right, and that was the trouble. I didn't know of anyone who had ever said a bad thing about the guy. That said a lot about the type of person that Mal Green had been.

"Had he run into any kind of trouble that you know of?"

"Wait, he did have a run in with a guy over at Captain Tony's place a couple of days ago, but he brushed it off when I asked about it."

"Do you remember the guy's name?"

"No, but Ken Bean might. Mal said he was bartending that night."

"I'll head there next and see what I can find out," I told her, standing.

"Thank you, Greg. It means a lot to me," Paloma said, standing on tip toes to kiss me softly on the lips. I wasn't sure what to say, so I said nothing. I smiled at her and headed for the door, getting while the getting was good.

I headed for Captain Tony's to talk to Ken Bean. Ken was a good guy and he knew practically everybody on the rock. If anybody knew who the guy was that Mal had gotten into it with, it would be Ken. This was certainly a lead of some kind.

Ken wasn't on duty yet when I got to Captain Tony's, so I ordered a beer and took a seat at the bar to wait. It was late afternoon and I was thankful to be inside and out of the sun. A glance at my watch told me it was near five, so Ken should be here soon unless something came up. Julie Moore was finishing up the day shift. She had heard about Mal Green, but didn't know anything about the guy that Mal had gotten into it with.

I finished my first beer and Julie had just placed a second next to my empty when Ken slipped in through the back. Ken was a bear of a man, covered with dark hair tinged with silver. When he worked, he doubled as a bouncer. Not too many people were willing to keeping causing problems once they got a look at him. His muscle shirt was stretched tightly across his barrel chest, and his arms were as big around as my thighs. I gave him a high sign and he came over. Julie told him she would stay and extra few minutes while we talked. Ken stepped around the bar and took a seat on the stool beside me.

"What can you tell about Mal Green and what happened last night?"

"Not much. The guy was drunk and bumped into Mal. Mal tried to diffuse it, but the guy wasn't having any of it. I split them up and sent the guy out. Mal stayed for another couple of hours and headed out just before the storm hit. I doubt that other guy hung around to wait for him," Ken explained.

"Okay, then it's back to the drawing board for me. Thank you, Ken. I dropped a ten on the bar and headed back to the crime scene. I had to have missed something. What was it?

Once I was back, I took a long look around, trying to figure out what I had missed. I could see where Mal had fallen after he had been struck. I looked around to see what else was there. That's when I saw it. The murder weapon. It had been there in plain sight all day. I had missed it before. I walked over and knelt down beside it. Yes, there was the blood. I pulled out my cellphone and dialed the Chief. Jamie answered on the first ring.

"Mal Green wasn't murdered," I told him.

"How do you know that?" he asked.

"Because I am looking right at the killer."

"What? You're confusing me."

"Remember the storm that blew through last night? How high the winds were?" I asked.

"Yes, I do," he replied.

"Mal was killed by a falling coconut. The one that hit him has blood on it. The wind shook it loose as he was walking under it. The coconut fell and the shell shattered his skull. Check with the

6

ME and tell him what I just told you. I'm pretty sure that he will confirm it," I told him.

This was a new one on me. Death by coconut. It was a coconut kill. I shook my head as I dialed Paloma Green to give her the news that her brother's death was an accident.

Coconuts falling from their trees and striking individuals can cause serious injury to the back, neck, shoulders and head, and are occasionally fatal.

Following a 1984 study on "Injuries Due to Falling Coconuts", exaggerated claims spread concerning the number of deaths by falling coconuts. Falling coconuts, according to urban legend, kill a few people a year. This legend gained momentum after the 2002 work of a noted expert on shark attacks was characterized as saying that falling coconuts kill 150 people each year worldwide. This statistic has often been contrasted with the number of shark-caused deaths per year, which is around five.

Concern about the risk of fatality due to falling coconuts led local officials in Queensland, Australia, to remove coconut trees from beaches in 2002. One newspaper dubbed coconuts "the killer fruit." Historical reports of actual death by coconut nonetheless date back to the 1770s.

Another way to "die by coconut" is to suffer sudden cardiac death as a result of hyperkalemia, after consuming moderate to large quantities of coconut water, due to the high levels of potassium in coconut water.

2. Four Fingers
Finds a Treasure

Shirrel Rhoades

Wharton Dalessandro was an ex-cop. But you wouldn't know it, watching him paint the old Marston house. Living here in Key West, he worked as a part-time house painter; that is, when he wasn't down on the dock in front of the Schooner Wharf Saloon playing chess with his buddy Dunk.

Dunk Reid was a fifth-generation Conch, as locals with a long family history are known here on the island that marks the far tip of the Florida Keys. His early ancestors were wreckers and pirates and scallywags, and this ill-gotten wealth had made Dunk a modern-day trust fund baby. He had nothing better to do than play chess with his friend Four Fingers (as Dalessandro was called due to a fishing mishap that lopped off a digit).

Dalessandro had been a homicide detective in New York City before getting put out to pasture after a few bullet wounds. So he'd retired to Key West for the easy life. Painting houses wasn't hard work when it came down to it. A way to make beer money.

This particular house – a three-story clapboard capped with a widow's watch providing an unobstructed view of the sea – had been built in 1833 by Captain John Mitchell Marston, one of the leaders in Commodore David Porter's Anti-Pirate Fleet. The West Indian Pirate Squadron was a group of ships commissioned by

President James Madison to curtail piracy in the Caribbean. Key West had been its home port.

As the historical marker at 625 Truman Avenue states:

PORTER'S ANTI-PIRATE FLEET

"An outbreak of piracy in 1822 prompted the United States to organize the West Indian Squadron, an anti-pirate fleet. Commanded by Commodore David Porter, the Squadron in 1823 included 17 ships and 1,100 men based in Key West. For two years the fleet attacked many of the estimated 2,000 pirates in the Indies. In 1825, after Porter was removed from command, Commodore Lewis Warrington continued the assault. Altogether 79 pirates were taken by U.S. ships."

In April 1823, Commodore Porter's "Mosquito Fleet" defeated a Cuban pirate known as Diabolito.

The Little Devil was a particularly dangerous pirate operating out of Cuba. Porter and his fleet cornered him off the northern coast of Cuba. The pirates abandoned their ship and fled inland. Some 30 of Diabolito's 70-man crew were killed or drowned. Diabolito escaped but was later encountered on his way to Yucatan and killed after he refused to surrender.

USS Montezuma – Capt. Marston's ship – was among those that captured Diabolito's 4-gun schooner. The *Catalina* was said to be loaded with treasure, but none was recovered. Some said it was lost at sea along with many of the pirates. You can't swim trying to carry gold chains and bouillon, someone pointed out.

That's why Four Fingers was taken aback when he found the box of silver coins tucked under the eaves of the roof. He was perched on a jerry-rigged stack of ladders, as precarious as a tightrope walker in a circus. His hand shook as he extracted the metal box from its hiding place. He didn't even notice when his bucket of paint slipped off its perch and went tumbling down, making a huge white splash on the front steps.

The heavy lockbox wedged under his arm, he managed to dial his pal Dunk on his iPhone. He had a clear view of the cell tower on Fleming Street from up here under the roof. "Hey Dunk, what do you do when you discover pirate treasure?" he blurted.

"Don't tell anybody," came the little man's advice. "Mel Fisher fought for eight years with the government over the gold he found at the wreck of the *Nuestra Señora de Atocha.*"

"But he won, right?"

"Eventually. But the Abandoned Shipwrecked Act of 1987 gives title for all shipwrecks within US waters to the United States and not to the discoverer of the shipwreck."

"But this wasn't found in US waters."

"You found it off the coast of Cuba?"

Four Fingers laughed. "You should know better than that. I'm right here on the island. You and I played chess just this morning at Schooner Wharf."

"Oh, right. So then where did you find this treasure?"

"At Capt. Marston's house on Caroline. I'm painting it."

"Humph, that's not good," Dunk snorted, his voice faint over the phone. "Eddie Marston owns that old pile of sticks. He'll claim it for himself, sure as shootin'."

"It's probably rightfully his. I found it under the eaves."

"Maybe he'll give you a reward. He's a little weasel, but he has kept his nose clean since he came home to claim the family manse after his auntie died last year."

"Yeah, it was Eddie who hired Pretty As Paint to touch up the house." The fixer-upper company was owned by Trixie Midas, his off-and-on girlfriend. If you ignored the tourist babes, pickings were limited on a 4-square-mile island.

"I'd know who to call if you found treasure offshore," said Dunk. "But on the island, I'm not sure."

"Think I'll call Johnny Leigh."

"The police chief?"

"Yeah," said Four Fingers. "I just opened the box. This isn't pirate treasure."

~ ~ ~

Chief Leigh ran his hands through the pile of coins. "Sure ain't pirate's doubloons," he said. "These are ordinary US coins — mostly quarters, some nickels and dimes. Must be a couple thousand dollars here."

"Those are mine," insisted Eddie Marston. "They were found on my property." He was a small guy, only an inch or two taller than Dunk Reid's 5-foot-2 height. He had a thin moustache that reminded you of a riverboat gambler. He wore a suit and tie despite the heat. One eye had a tic, like a shorted neon light.

"Yes, but did you put the box here yourself?" asked Four Finger, cocking his head as he waited for the answer.

"Course I did. It's my money."

Four Fingers turned to Chief Leigh. "Arrest this man," he said casually.

"W-what for?" stuttered Eddie Marston.

"I hear you have a record for B&E," shrugged Four Fingers Dalessandro. His friend Dunk had filled him in on Eddie's shady past.

"So what? I did my time, paid my debt to society."

"But you didn't get caught for this one."

"What are you talking about?" snapped Chief Johnny Leigh, having trouble following the back-and-forth.

"Simple. Eddie's a crook. This money was hidden away so it's probably stolen. It's all coins, so it probably came from that Acme Vending Machine robbery up in Jacksonville a few years back. Vending machines take coins. That burglary was never solved."

"What makes you think the money came from there?" asked Chief Leigh.

"That robbery took place in 1999, a few years after I moved to Key West. That's why I remember it, still in my policing mode. And none of the coins in that box are dated later than 1999. So congratulations, Johnny, you've cracked the case."

"Wait, I didn't do that job alone," said Eddie Marston. "Go easy on me and I'll give you the other names."

"Likely Leon Midas," shrugged Four Fingers.

"How did you know that?" said Eddie. Surprised by the man's acuity.

"I sometimes date Penny Midas, Leon's ex-wife. She's told me he used to pal around with you before he got sent to Raiford. Birds of a feather and all that. He was probably your partner in crime. You both lived in Jacksonville in 1999, according to Penny."

"Ain't fair," grumbled Eddie. "That money's been hidden there in the rafters for more'n twenty years and you have to stumble on it."

"Hey, you hired me to paint your house."

"Well, you can forget about that. You're fired."

"Then you can clean up that white paint I spilled on your steps. I'm not doing it."

3. Pauline's Closet

Rusty Hodgson
(A/K/A Rusty the Writer)

"I'm telling you. I'm not exaggerating. There's something up there."

Sally had never seen Ryan so agitated. Or was it just pure excitement? "What did you see?"

"Well, it was very dark. But I definitely saw the outline of edges, like of boxes, maybe even some furniture."

Sally was astounded. Ryan had come to her two weeks before telling her about the closet and that he wanted to see what was inside. It was located above the door leading into the boys' bedroom. "You're not going to get into any trouble, are you? We need you to keep this job."

Ryan had landed the position as a tour guide at the Hemingway Home and Museum in Key West a year ago. He loved it. He was a natural, his red hair and green eyes tantalizing the females, young and old. He was just as adept at communicating his love of literature and Ernest Hemingway as he was at dealing with the idiosyncrasies of the tourists who inundated the place on a daily basis.

"Nah. I'm being very careful. But I've got to get up there and take a longer look."

"How are you going to do that? Oh shit, Ryan. You're going to get caught and we're going to be sleeping at KOTS with the homeless."

Ryan had always liked how Sally looked when she became concerned. Her normally unwrinkled brow puckered as if kissing the air, her deep dimples quivered. "I won't get in trouble. I've got it all figured out."

Sally knew better than to convince Ryan to step back and reconsider his plan. That would just set his resolve in concrete no jackhammer could extricate. "Okay, but be careful," was all she could say.

~ ~ ~

Ryan hadn't noticed the door until a month into his job. He had spent weeks studying the script, walking the property with a seasoned tour guide, and reading up on every tidbit of arcane information about the property and Hemingway he could find. No one had mentioned it. It was smallish, about 4' by 3', situated weirdly just above the door leading from Patrick and Gregory's room to their nanny's. At a height of 7', it was inaccessible without a ladder.

The upstairs of the house sported 12' ceilings. The area between the two rooms was strangely wide, about 4', and there was a ground floor closet to the right of the doorway. Ryan had seen its interior once, and noted that the closet's ceiling was of normal height.

Some of the museum's guests would ask what was up there, and since Ryan was often also questioned about whether the place was haunted, he'd joke that it was where they kept the ghost of Ernest Hemingway. But inexorably, he was attracted to the space as if by a human magnet. What was up there?

He had to see for himself. He had told Sally he was just going to try to get the door open. And that was the truth. Two tour guides a day are designated the "late" guides, and as such, they are responsible for staying until 5:30 to make sure all guests have left the property and the home is secured by checking the lights and setting the alarm.

He went back into the home on the chosen day, retrieved the stepladder he knew that housekeeping used to clean chandeliers and other hard-to-reach places, and climbed to the level of the door. It did not take long to whittle around and pry the door open with a large screwdriver. It was then with the small flashlight he brought that he was able to see what he had related to Sally. Of course, that just whetted his interest.

~ ~ ~

It was on a typically hot humid early evening in August that Ryan launched his plan to explore further. This time he used a light attached to his head by a strap so as to free his hands. It only took a few minutes to re-open the door. He was shaking with anticipation as he squeezed his 6' frame into the opening. The light barely pierced the

dust mites that danced feverishly in the gloom. He noticed his were the

only footsteps in the half-inch or so of dust on the floor.

He first saw the side of a small, squat chest of drawers, ornate gold-colored engravings around the rusted pulls. Next a stand-up lamp, fluted and possibly bronze, with no shade. These, by their relatively newer design, Ryan surmised were additional pieces of furniture used at some time since the home had been turned into a museum. Hunching over because of the low ceiling, he hit his head on a cross-beam. Soon he discovered it was the banister to a tiny staircase that led to an upper level only feet above. Almost crawling up the stairs, he whinnied his way up to this area. Scanning it by turning his head back and forth, he saw a small suitcase, about the size of a modern-day carry-on, over in a corner, no more than 6' away. It was the only visible object.

He crawled over to the case and dragged it back to the first level where there was a little more headroom. In the dim light, he could see it was leather, the skin now dried and mottled with age. The snap clasps were rusted shut, so he used the screwdriver to pry them open. The smell of decay almost made him gag. He directed his light inside, and saw hundreds of sheets of paper, the sides tattered and partially dissolving. Some were carbon dark blue, most a parchment color. Hesitantly he pulled out one sheet.

He immediately recognized it as the beginning of the story entitled "The Big Two-Hearted River," part of the Nick Adam's stories. It had been typed on an antique typewriter, the letters slightly listing to one side or the other. His hands quivered as he pulled out more pages, all from the stories. A second grouping were carbon copies of the first. How did these get here? Then Ryan recalled the well-known story:

The autumn of 1922 was difficult for Hadley and Ernest, who had been married just over a year and were living in Paris. Ernest was a foreign correspondent for the Toronto Star, writing about everything from trout fishing and meeting Mussolini to inflation and the German currency. In September, Ernest was directed to go to Constantinople to write about the war raging between Greece and Turkey. It was a difficult assignment, made more challenging because Hadley did not want him to go. It was the first serious rift in their marriage, and Hadley was so adamant about his not going that they were not speaking to each other when he left. On that trip, Ernest was gone for a month and Hadley stayed in Paris. When Ernest returned, he was miserably sick with malaria and covered in bug bites.

On November 22, less than a month later, Ernest was sent to Lausanne Switzerland to write about the Peace conference in Geneva. Hadley stayed behind to nurse her cold, but Ernest wrote several letters, urging her to join him as soon as she was well. Finally, in the first week of December, she made plans to go to Switzerland. After the conference, they planned to go on to Blonay-Chamby. As Hadley packed for the trip, she thought to bring Ernest's works in progress so that he could share them with Lincoln Steffens, whom he had just met. She packed Ernest's manuscripts, including the carbon copies, in a small overnight valise. These were early Nick Adam's stories about Michigan, the short stories Ernest had been working on for months. As she boarded the train at Gare de Lyon, the station in Paris.

What happened next is, of course, legend. Hadley found her place on the train, stowed her bags, and went to buy water before the train left the station. When she returned, the small overnight bag was gone. Hadley sought help from the conductor and although they searched the train, the manuscripts could not be found. It was a long train ride for Hadley, who had to tell Ernest "such a thing", when she reached her destination.

Ernest wrote in *A Movable Feast*:

"I had never seen anyone hurt by a thing other than death or unbearable suffering except Hadley when she told me about the things being gone. She had cried and cried and could not tell me. I told her that no matter what the dreadful thing was that had happened nothing could be that bad, and whatever it was, it was all right and not to worry. We could work it out. Then, finally, she told me. I was sure she could not have brought the carbons too and I hired someone to cover for me on my newspaper job. I was making good money then at journalism, and took the train for Paris. It was true all right and I remember what I did in the night after I let myself into the flat and found it was true."

Searching further inside the suitcase, stuck in a far corner, Ryan located an envelope, browned, but newer than the pages. It simply said, *"Open it if you must,"* written in longhand on the outside. Ryan carefully opened it. It was a short letter, in the same hand as the envelope. It read:

I realize history will judge me harshly. But I was at that party in Oak Park when Ernest first met Hadley. I had known of her in St. Louis. I was infatuated immediately with the young man they called Ernest, but he paid me no heed, devoting his full attention to Hadley.

I was in Paris in 1922 on a vacation. When I arrived I learned Ernest was in Switzerland, but also heard through a confidential source that Hadley was planning on visiting him from Paris. From the same source I learned which train and the time. I didn't know quite what I was going to do, but just needed to derail the trip in some way. When I saw her leave her compartment, I hopped aboard. She had several suitcases, but one was smaller, likely to contain her toiletries, so I grabbed it and ran.

You now see what was contained in that valise. I was horror struck when I first saw it. Could it possibly be the only copies of Ernest's works? Now I know I should have immediately sent them to him, But I could only imagine his ire at Hadley for losing them. Over the years of my marriage to him, I wanted to tell him so many times, that the original drafts of his great work were only feet above our bed. If you have read this letter, these are now yours. Do what you want with them. My guilty conscience is intertwined among the pages.

I was incapable of moving. My heart pounded against my ribs. What was I going to do with this? What were these documents worth?

I sat in silence for an interminable time. I think I fell asleep. Suddenly I heard the outside sounds of the housekeeping staff. I had to get out quickly. I left the suitcase and the opened letter just as I had found them, exited the closet door, scurried down the ladder and took my leave from the building just as two cleaning women came around the corner. They looked surprised at my presence so early in the morning, but said nothing about it.

When I arrived home I found all of Sally's possessions missing. Cleaned out. Not a trace. There was a note on the bed.

You stayed out all night without calling. I can only imagine where you were. We're done. Don't contact me. No calls, texts, no messages. Nothing.
-Sally

I didn't blame her. My discovery had changed me. I had only one goal in life: to figure out what to do with the suitcase and papers. I decided I had to get the valise out of the closet and store it elsewhere safely. I arrived at work very early the next morning.

I was shaking with expectation when I placed the ladder up to the closet. When I stepped up into the area, I immediately noticed a fresh pair of footsteps in the dust, parallel to mine. But smaller. Then I saw that the valise was no longer in the place I had left it. I searched frantically around the entire area. No suitcase. Then, out of the corner of my eye, I caught the corner of an envelope sticking from a crevice formed by one of the rafters. I tore it open. It read:

I took these back. Sorry. It was time. Have a great day.
-Pauline

4. Will and Betsy Black Solve a Murder

David Beckwith

Will and Betsy were sitting at the bar with their friends and neighbors, Art and Carol Joye, in the Square Grouper waiting for a table. As usual it was packed and since the Square Grouper didn't take reservations, a wait during peak dinner hours was almost inevitable. But the wait was worth it since they would get an excellent meal.

As they sat at the bar unwinding and rehashing the day, Jake Blanchard entered and started looking around the room, making a mental inventory of who was there.

The rest of his party ordered wine and then went to wait out front until their table was ready. Jake, however, saw Will and Betsy and elbowed his way through the crowd to where they were sitting.

"Hi, neighbor," Will said. "Thanks from us as well as Neil Dixon's widow for caring enough to sponsor the benefit. I think everyone had a very successful and memorable day, and we both know the benefit proceeds will come in real handy."

"Thanks. Yeah! It was a success, wasn't it? Everyone had a good time, and it was for a good cause, too. It turned out to be one God demined good party. I got snockered before the day was out," Jake said. "It's too bad Geoffrey Watson couldn't have been there with us."

"We heard Geoffrey was very active in rounding up volunteers for the event," Betsy said.

"Yes, he was. What have you heard about the investigation into his death?" Jake probed.

"Oh, I'm sure the same things you've heard - what's been reported in the newspaper," Will said.

Jake looked skeptical. "With your connections, I'm sure you know more than us Joe-blows on the street. After all, you're the ones who found him, aren't you?"

"Unfortunately, we did call it in," Will said.

"You didn't investigate Watson's boat?" Jake said. "Shit, I would've wanted to know what had happened."

"We just secured a line to the boat so it wouldn't drift off and waited for the authorities," Will said.

"You didn't see anything suspect?" Jake asked suspiciously.

"No, Jake, we really didn't. I guess we were too shocked to give it much thought."

"You're sure you didn't see anything incriminating?" Jake pressed. "The fuzz didn't tell you to keep your trap shut, did they?"

"Why the in-depth interest?" Will said, starting to get a little irritated. "Was Geoffrey Watson something to you? Is there something suspicious we should have noticed?"

"Of course not. How would I know? I wasn't there. I'd been at the fund raiser for hours," Blanchard said, starting to get defensive. "I guess I'm just overreacting because I found the scene disturbing, and it put a damper on my day of fun in the sun. Or maybe it shook me up because he was in a Hades boat. Hey, I barely knew the guy, and I've never done business with him. Don't let me take up any more of your time. You have a good dinner. I'd better rejoin my party out front before our table buzzer goes off. Good to see you again. By the way, got a business card? Let's keep in touch."

He shook hands and abruptly left.

"I wonder what that was all about," Betsy said after his departure.

Will shrugged.

"You heard him say he'd never done any business with Watson. It said in Miracle Key's promotional brochure that the ferry going back and forth to Miracle Key is a craft specially designed for them by Hades Boats."

Art and Carol were listening to Jake Blanchard's comments.

Art turned to Will and Betsy and said, "Did you hear Jake say he was upset because Watson's body was found on a Hades boat? I don't remember seeing that detail in the newspaper. Did you?"

"Now that you mention it, I don't think that fact was included," Will said.

With quizzical looks, Kim and Betsy shook their heads in agreement.

Had Will and Betsy just solved a crime?

5. Mendy's Exit

Earl Smith

Monique and I had spent a romantic weekend at the Plaza Hotel in Manhattan. We did take time off to touch base with an assistant UN ambassador from the UK, who isn't really a diplomat. Monique wasn't cleared to fly solo for such briefings, but she was catching on fast. Particularly for someone who hadn't spent years in the intelligence game. I kissed her goodbye and headed for LaGuardia and the Gulfstream. She took the Excella to DC and her first, low-risk assignment. Getting to know certain shady types from Langley. A sexy French woman against a bunch of James Bond wannabees! They wouldn't have a chance.

I landed at Key West International Airport and grabbed a cab to the compound on Southard Street. I was looking forward to a relaxing time and recharging. The other two women were in Geneva delivering updates on the Svetlana/Bob episode. They wouldn't return for a couple of days. So, I had the place to myself. Well, that's not totally true. Kurt and Jeremy were patrolling and manning the gatehouse. Chang was seeing to the grounds. Mae Lee was preparing the kitchen for a mass arrival. She always looked forward to getting the whole family together.

Kurt and Jeremy came as a matched set. Both were Seal Team. alumni. They'd met during an action in Africa and fell in love. They were sent in my direction when they decided to exit. The guys provide security for the compound and manage its various defensive capabilities.

Chang and Mae Lee are also a couple. They came to me through contacts in China. He's a master gardener. She manages the house and is a chef extraordinaire. Both are past operatives and dangerous in close combat situations.

Then there's the other two women. Mary is a Scottish lass who, through a series of extraordinary happenings, spent years working as a field operative for the Germans. She's fluent in six languages, a crack shot and a demon with a knife. Her advantage is her classic beauty. Five ten, appropriately curvy, and a face that speaks of solid confidence, but hints at a wild side. Devilish grin, that one has. Add in her red hair and sea green eyes. She is what one of my old mentors used to describe as "a woman far too dangerous to be considered beautiful." She is both, by the way.

Angelique is the youngster of the group. She grew up in Paris. Worked as an undercover operative for Interpol in the drug trafficking and organized crime divisions for about two decades. Never held a desk job. Half Vietnamese and half French, five six, slim, almost boyish. Wears her jet-black hair short. A wonderful combination of Asian demure and intense French femininity. Easy to underestimate. Many have to their misfortune. One of the most devious women I've ever met. She can find your back door and own your entire house before you even begin to suspect there's a threat. She's short of double-digits. Just eight kills. Another dangerous woman.

Like Monique and me, both are classified immortal. We travel in the open and are, at least in theory, immune from attack. Should one be attempted, retribution would be sharply forthcoming from several different directions. We who travel under titanium umbrellas. Part of the perks of the business I'm in.

Svetlana and Bob are in the last month of their isolation on Anna's island off the north coast of Cuba. They have behaved themselves and are due to return to Southard next month. I sent a minister down to perform a certain ceremony. Afterwards, he presented Svetlana with her very own US passport. Told her she was now an American citizen. He said she cried. And that's something from a double-digit operative with more than ten kills.

I spent a couple delightful hours in the backyard and soaking in the hot tub. Then retired to a hammock to catch up on much-needed sleep. As much preparing for what I knew was coming as recovering from the weekend in Manhattan. One woman can wear you out. Three can be a challenge. Especially if they've been away for a while.

I headed upstairs to prepare for dinner and was just stepping out of the shower when the secure phone rang. Whenever I'm dripping wet and that happens, my gut tightens. This time my gut was right.

"Hey John," said a voice that I immediately recognized.

"Okay Ralph, don't tell me you're about to ruin the first relaxing day I've had in a while."

"Sorry buddy. I know you're probably up to your neck in women, but this is important."

"Damn your eyes. If you must know, I'm a bachelor for a couple of days. Monique is in DC probing a few spooks. Mary and Angelique are in Geneva briefing the same. Other than the staff, I've got the place to myself. I was just starting to shift into Key West mode. And you're going to piss on my campfire, right?"

"We need your help with another exit," Ralph said. "This one may be a bit dicey."

Over the next few minutes, he gave me the basics. A woman, codenamed Mendy, was a highly productive operative for British intelligence. What made it dicey was that she also had connections into the mafia in London. She'd been a very reliable source of information on both Chinese activities and a certain Russian mob boss. But, over the last few months, she'd made it increasingly clear that she wanted out. Get her out or a tell-all book. Quid pro quos were in the air.

That's where I came in. My specialty is turning actives into neutrals. The first exit involved getting out Svetlana, a Russian field operative, and Bob, a CIA operative turned desk driver. The two wanted to be one and that was driving both sides nuts. It turned out to be a tricky undertaking, which I've described in a prior missive. But I was successful. They are now Mister and Misses and semi-officially out of the business.

I did take my pound of flesh as part of that deal. Ownership of the compound on Southard, unquestioned sanction ability, Key West designated permanently neutral ground, a reliable source of unquestioned funding and the ability to build my own team. in anticipation of similar requests. Homebase is a large two-story house set well back from the road. It has a guest cottage, pool house, and guardhouse. The tech guys have wired it to the max and installed an impressive range of defensive capabilities.

After my conversation with Ralph, I asked Kurt and Jeremy to ratchet up security a bit. Nothing imminent but knocking the rust off seemed prudent. We hadn't had any real action for several months. I let Mae Lee know that we were about to have extra company and that it was time to get the larder stocked. Instructed the team. on Anna's island that Svetlana and Bob were going to be released early. Then two more phone calls, one to DC and another to Geneva. Monique, Mary, and Angelique would arrive tomorrow.

I got a good night's sleep. I always do before an action. In the morning, I filled in some of the details for the staff. The danger that the compound would be attacked was minimal. The network of agreements with various intelligence agencies saw to that. The trick was getting Mendy onto Key West and into my presence alive. If we could manage that, she would be safely under my protection. But she would be fair game until that occurred.

Monique was taking the American Airlines nonstop from DCA. She would arrive just before noon and head directly to the compound. Mary and Angelique were taking the Gulfstream. to

Lauderdale, then on to Key West. They would land around two in the afternoon. I asked them to check sources once they arrived. Identify any suspicious arrivals. Then head for the compound. I expected them at Southard a couple of hours before dinner.

I'm know some of you are curious about certain arrangements. So let me address the prurient questions right up front. The back half of the top floor of the house has a master bedroom with a large circular bed, a lounging area with a dining table and a large bathroom complete with a spa and shower that will hold four. The front half of the floor contains three private bedrooms, one for each of the girls. So, yes. Two or more of us more than occasionally...

That being said, there's a bit less sex involved than you might imagine. The bonds among us are very strong and we sleep comfortably in each other's company. Just like cobras that sleep more soundly in the presence of other cobras. We completely relax because any clown dumb enough to disturb our sleep would be dead nine times before he hit the floor.

In anticipation of the arrivals, I gave Mae Lee her marching orders. "Beginning at five and through until eight the next morning, the upper floor is closed. Set up dinner by five o'clock. Two dozen oysters with champagne." Here the demure Mae Lee cleared her throat. "Okay, make it three dozen and four bottles of champagne. For the main course, pompano encrust, Lobster MacGregor, the nice Spanish white, and a dessert which is not too sticky. Breakfast at the normal time. Late brunch in the garden at one thirty tomorrow afternoon. Expect two extras." She giggled as she walked away.

Back in the office, more details from Ralph had arrived. Mendy was hot. The word was out. Bird in flight. She had made it to Madrid where the Spanish and Brits had combined to get her to a safe house in Barcelona. The wild card wasn't the Chinese. Sure, they might try to take her out before she got to me. That was their option. But they had signed onto the agreement which established the exit door. The bigger problem was the crime boss and, more importantly, his youngest son. A hothead who had developed the hots for Mendy. They were not party to the agreements.

The Spaniards got Mendy out of Barcelona successfully. From there she was flown to the Azores, handed over to the Portuguese, then on to Cuba. ETA Key West twelve hours give or take.

The deep-encrypt sang its sweet song, telling me that a message had come in. I read it with some relief. The Chinese had acknowledged that Mendy was heading for the exit and made it clear that, if I was to provide the appropriate assurances, they would not try to take her out. Not particularly happy about it but resigned. They did ask for access to any information she might deliver on a certain mob boss. That was to be expected and ignored. They had to try to salvage something out of a bad situation. Now we were down to the black sheep of the mob family and his embarrassed godfather father.

Monique arrived shortly after noon. Her eyes grew wide as I told her what was going down. The only questions she asked were about her role. I like that about her. I answered, reassured, and then sent her down to the range in the basement to refresh her skills with a handgun. Kurt went along as instructor.

A text message told me that Mary and Angelique had arrived at Lauderdale, were having the Gulfstream. refueled, and would be touching base with our local sources once they arrived in the Conch Republic. They expected to be at the compound by three. Angelique wanted to know if there would be oysters for dinner.

Mary tossed the next log on the fire. It seems that the younger had sent two hotheads on ahead and they were presently in Key West setting up an ambush. From what she and Angelique could gather, their marching orders were to capture Mendy and present her as a trophy. I triggered a sanction with the instructions to ice them, but I left open the option of HWC. That's code for Halfway to Cuba. Having them on ice might be a useful bargaining chip if his kid didn't survive and the godfather decided to go to war.

Then came the information that the Don's younger son was on the move. He had left London, landed in Barcelona and was being indiscreet in his inquiries. The first information came indirectly from his father, who was obviously concerned that his son's passion for Mendy would turn out to be all-consuming. The Spanish picked up the latter. Apparently, it wasn't difficult. They'd learned that he had booked a flight to Miami and then chartered a plane through to Key West. I arranged a welcoming committee.

Ninety minutes later, I received notification that the sanction had been carried out. The two were drinking at Irish Kevin's when Mary and Angelique got them to buy a round of drinks. Two drops in each of those and they were highly malleable zombies. The girls walked them out of the bar and into a Land Rover. In less than thirty minutes they were on Wisteria Island trying to figure out what the hell happened. I got a text from Angelique. "Two on ice. Rank amateurs. Too easy, Drill Sergeant!" She was going to be a sassy handful tonight.

The mini-Don arrived in Key West and made a rookie mistake. The lady who was managing the taxis made sure he got into a certain cab. They headed across the bridge and up to our country house on Big Pine Key. They got to the top of Stock Island before the junior jackass realized they were going in the wrong direction. A mist from an aerosol put him out. He woke up in a padded cell. The text they sent me read, "One on ice and dumb as a stump. Hold him or HWC?" My response was, "Continue icing, no swimming lessons until I say so. Daddy is sure to call."

Mary and Angelique arrived at Southard on schedule and settled in for a hen fest with Monique. I've lived with two or more women several times during my life and found it very comfortable. One of the major benefits is that they have each other to talk to about things I find either boring or irritating. If you throw in a couple of gay boyfriends guarding the gate, it makes for a very happy covey of quail. They spent the next hour catching up and telling tales.

Svetlana and Bob arrived halfway through the hen fest. After hugs, handshakes, and the obligatory ring viewing, I briefed them on what was going down. Their role was simple. They would sit on the porch, in plain sight, as evidence they were under my protection. Both would be armed but act only if the situation demanded. Briefing completed, I had Jeremy take them to the guest cottage. Mae Lee would see to their needs until brunch the next afternoon. I got a smile and a wink from Svetlana as she nodded towards the three up on the porch.

The reunion over dinner was a delight on all fronts. The pompano was a masterpiece, the Lobster MacGregor was stuffed and in the shell, the wine was superb. And we got through the dessert without messing the bed linens. Later, the boosts from the oysters and champaign were put to excellent use. And then we slept soundly and deeply, peacefully secure in each other's company. The sun rose over a very satisfied bedroom.

The next morning, with breakfast digesting, I was sitting with Mary and Angelique at the table in what we referred to as the launching pad, waiting for Mendy to show up. It's a walled area just inside the main gate with a round table and four chairs. We use it for visitors who are unwelcome in the main complex. Anyone who enters can be very well covered from both the gatehouse and the upper floor of the main house. There's also a hide against the far-right wall. It was Monique's turn in the hole, as we call it. Well shielded by vegetation, heavily armored, and designed to disguise the twelve-gauge shotgun double barrel, it could produce a nasty surprise for anyone who made a serious mistake.

Kurt and Jeremy had picked Mendy up at the ferry terminal from Fort Jefferson in the Dry Tortugas. From the Azores, we had flown her to Havana. Then put her on a floatplane to the truly southernmost point of American territory. Now, on Key West, she was heading for the compound.

We had it choreographed down to the minute. Kurt and Jeremy brought Mendy through the front gate. I got mugged. She broke away from them, wrapped her arms around me and began to cry. After she settled down, I held her at arm's length and told her what was about to happen.

"You have no lines. You will be a no danger. Other than what you might create for yourself. We are about to have a visitor. You will recognize him and he you. He will ask for assurances, and I will give them. I will then ask if we are in accord. If he agrees that we are, you no longer belong to him but to me. For as long as I require, you will follow my instructions without exception. You will not disagree, argue, grumble or grouse. Eventually, and solely at my discretion, you will become a neutral. Is that clear?"

She took a step backwards and nodded. "Now stand on my right side behind the chair. You will not speak or move until I tell you. No matter how frightened you might become, you must believe that you are completely safe, and that no harm can come to you. If our visitor asks you a question or speaks to you in any way, you will not respond. In fact, you will not react in any way. If you violate these instructions, our deal is off, and you are on your own. I will see that you are safely off the island but do no more. Do you understand and agree?" She nodded a second time and moved around behind me.

Jeremy headed to the second floor of the guardhouse. He would take up a position that would put him above and behind our visitor and with a clear view of the street outside. Kurt got Svetlana and Bob settled on the porch. He would serve as gatekeeper. Mary and Angelique headed for the balcony on the second floor of the main house. Shielded and with long guns, they had a direct line of sight. And, if that was not enough, the field stones that our visitor would be standing on during our short meeting were undergirded with explosives. We've never tested it, but the tech guys tell me that it would get him fully a third of the way to Cuba if I threw the switch.

The sound of a car pulling up outside the gate told us that our visitor was arriving. The device under the table buzzed softly three times as Jeremy indicated that our guest had brought two associates. Kurt would enforce the rules. Only one was to be allowed in, and then unarmed. It would be the first test of our arrangement with the Chinese.

After a short, and sometimes heated, conversation in Mandarin – Kurt is fluent – an elderly gentleman came through the gate and onto the launching pad. A single buzz from Jeremy told me that things were calm on the street.

The visitor shot a hard look at Mendy. I could feel her tense up and then relax. "Your business here is with me and not with her. Are we agreed?"

He took a step forward towards one of the chairs, but Kurt made it clear that he would be standing not sitting. Ever the perfectionist, Kurt returned him precisely to the launching pad. He slowly nodded his head and said, "I have been told that you are immortal. You must feel very confident in that. Requiring only a single insurance policy."

"Twenty percent is not a very good start." A look of uncertainty briefly crossed his face. And then he smiled. "But to be honest," I continued, "the others are only for training purposes. You and I both know that, should you, or any of your people, misbehave, none of you would leave the island alive and each member of your extensive organization would have a new target on their back. We both know you are not going to risk that. The issues that we must settle are two. First, that you will undertake not to interfere with the process of removing this woman from the game. Second, that you will accept my undertakings in this matter."

"And what if your undertakings are unsuccessful?"

"Then I will remove my protection. She will be eliminated. I will notify you of the event. Provide proof as required. I assume you find that acceptable." He nodded slowly, glanced at Mendy, and then bowed stiffly.

"Are we in accord," I asked?

"We are in accord," he replied.

"Then I bid you a good day. As I understand it, you have a private plane at the airport. I request that you and your associates depart the island at your earliest convenience. Kurt will return your weapon as you leave."

With our visitor gone, Mendy relaxed. She was surprised when Monique and the twelve-gauge emerged from the hole and then again when Jeremy, Mary and Angelique showed up armed. "You weren't bluffing when you said twenty percent."

I nodded towards Svetlana and Bob on the porch. "It was less than twenty percent. I never bluff." Then I got stern. "Here's what's going to happen. You will spend the next six months on an island off the north coast of Cuba. You will not be a prisoner and will have every opportunity to communicate with anyone you wish. But, if you attempt to contact anyone - I repeat, anyone - in the business, our deal will be off. And you have heard what will happen." She nodded slowly. "If anyone in the business attempts to contact you, you will report it immediately and without responding to their attempt. We will handle it from there. Do you understand?"

"I was hoping to stay here with you." I shot her a hard glance. She dropped her eyes and said, "I will do as you say. I put my life in your hands. You have my word on it."

Mae Lee announced that brunch would be served in half an hour. Jeremy and Kurt headed for the Gatehouse. There's a bedroom and full bath on the first floor. Mendy was sent in to freshen up. Svetlana and Bob went to the Guest Cottage to do the same. The four of us headed upstairs for a group shower and fresh change of clothes.

Brunch in the garden was an informal affair. It was a celebration of sorts. But I could see that Mendy was focused on the months before her. The girls did their best to get her thinking on other things.

As Mae Lee and Chang were clearing the table, I turned to Jeremy and nodded towards Mendy. "Take her to the airport. The Cessna will be waiting." Then to Mendy, "You are on trial, but I trust your pledge. Follow the rules and things will work out." They headed out together.

Mae Lee came to let me know that I was wanted on the phone. A gravelly voice with a heavy Russian accent said, "I understand you have something that belongs to me."

"Actually, I have three things that belong to you."

After a long pause, he continued, "The other two are of no interest to me. You can do with them as you wish. I am asking that you return my son to my care."

"I appreciate your frankness and will deliver the same in return. Your family is not a party to the networks of agreements which protect my organization. However, in the past you have evidenced prudence by not invading my interests. Because of that, I'm prepared to accept that the actions of your youngest son were neither ordered nor approved by you."

Again, a pause. "Your assumption is correct. My son's actions are an embarrassment to the family. I have no quarrel with you, nor do I seek one. My sole interest in this matter is to recover my son. We do not know each other so you have no basis to judge what I am about to say. He will not fare well if you return him to me. Short of ending his life, there is nothing you can do to him which will be as severe and punishing as what I plan."

"I am prepared to deliver him into your care if we can reach agreement on two issues. Firstly, neither myself nor any member of my family will ever come under attack as a result of your orders or actions. Secondly, you will accept and agree to the general provisions of the agreements which have established and maintained my efforts."

This time there was no pause. "You have my word on both accounts."

"It is my understanding that your son has charted a plane which is presently at the Key West airport. We will make delivery and there will be no attempt to track the aircraft once it leaves. Please alert the pilot." I ended the call and gave instructions to the crew on Big Pine Key.

My next call was to Ralph. "I have a gift for you. Two young, and fairly inept, members of the Godfathers family. I think you may have a use for them. I do not. I'll have them delivered to Gitmo. But I need a favor in return. I'm sure you can find an appropriate gift in one of the federal storage warehouses. Something Catholic and meaningful. Have it delivered to the Godfather with my compliments. Further, it would be useful if you asked the Brits to interrupt harassment for a few weeks." He wanted to know details, but I would only tell him that they might be forthcoming at some future date.

The next morning, I sat down with Svetlana and Bob and arranged for their new home. They are living in the high desert in a grand house and with the fat bank account.

Two weeks later, a van pulled up in front of the compound and delivered twenty cases of top-of-the-line Russian caviar and as many cases of fine Russian vodka. One of the cans of caviar and two of the bottles of vodka formed the core of a celebratory dinner in the master bedroom. Most of both were consumed. We did make a mess that got Mae Lee clucking.

6. Walter the Weirdo Gets His Just Dessert

H.L. Osterman

Walter de Worcester was homeless. But if you were going to be living on the street, Key West was a good place to do it. The hottest it had ever been was 95° F; the coldest 41° – but the temperature rarely falls below 67° or exceeds 82°. Comfortable on most days. Good for outdoor living.

Walter liked it.

Walter de Worcester used to be a successful attorney, but circumstances had not gone in his favor. After being disbarred (never mind the details), he moved to the tip end of Florida, taking up residence on the streets of the Southernmost City in the Continental United States.

There's a reason other than Mile Marker 0 at the end of US 1 that Key West is known as an end-of-the-road town. It's where you go when there's nowhere left to go.

Although not exactly welcomed, the vagrant population in Key West is plentiful. As that Michael McCloud song proclaims, *"I'd rather be here just drinking a beer than be freezing my ass in the North."*

Walter wasn't normal, anybody could tell you that. He nearly fell off the autism spectrum, somewhere near *Rain Man* status. If you wanted to be kind, you might call him an *idiot savant* – but the emphasis was likely to be on *idiot*.

People called him Walter the Weirdo.

The name suited him, for he had an ability to solve murders with ease, some sort of mental calculations that even he couldn't explain.

According to medical books, "Savant syndrome is a rare condition in which someone with significant mental disabilities demonstrates certain abilities far in excess of average. The skills that savants excel at are generally related to memory. This may include rapid calculations, artistic ability, map making, or musical ability.apple-wikipedia-api://en.wikipedia.org/w/api.php?action=parse&redirects&prop=text%7Cdisplaytitle&format=xml&page=Idiot_savant&apple_local_param=21-com.apple.DictionaryApp.Wikipedia - cite_note-Tref2009-1 Usually, only one exceptional skill is present."

Walter's skill was solving crimes.

Randall Ray Raymond, Monroe County's sheriff, had long recognized the little man's ability, but he avoided contact as much as possible. Putting Walter on the stand was a sure way to lose a court case. Juries would be confused by the man's rambling testimony and quirky behavior.

When Sheriff Raymond's deputies got a call about a body spotted in the mangroves off Big Cow Key, he was tempted to ask Walter's opinion. However, he quickly thought better of it. The little nutjob's insights were often helpful, but he was a public relations nightmare. The last time he'd called on Walter de Worcester, a headline in the Key West *Citizen* had proclaimed:

SHERIFF RECRUITS HOMELESS MAN AS INVESTIGATOR.

Never mind that Walter identified the culprit within ten minutes of shuffling around the crime scene, the fallout was nonetheless damaging to Randy Raymond's professional reputation. The County Sheriff is an elected position. His political rivals made the most of this seemingly irresponsible behavior.

For a while after that, the sheriff became the butt of local jokes:

How many homeless men does it take to solve a crime?

Only one – Sheriff Raymond who will be homeless after the next election!

The body found in the mangrove turned out to be a local fisherman named Buddy Boy Benson. Nobody knew what he'd been doing up near Big Cow Key. The fishing's not particularly good up there due to pollutants from a sunken tanker. They don't mention things like this in the tourist brochures. The ship had been carrying some kind of chemicals. The EPA was supposed to clean up the area, but governmental wheels turn slowly.

Buddy Boy's wife said he had a charter that day, some vacationers from Ohio hoping to pull in a few groupers. And drink beer. Buddy Boy's boat – the *Saint Louis Shuffle* – had a battery-powered Igloo cooler that kept Budweisers at a near-freezing temperature. Perfect for a hot day. And yesterday the thermometer had read 94°.

Nobody remembers seeing Buddy Boy's charter group. Sam Elkins, who berthed his boat next to the *Saint Louis Shuffle*, said it left the dock without any passengers or crew. John Bethell's oldest boy Floyd usually served as First Mate when the *Saint Louis Shuffle* had a charter. But he had been in Miami with his dad buying a new pickup, a Ford F-150.

Sheriff Raymond couldn't make heads nor tails of it. His deputies had turned up no clues. Heck, they couldn't even find Buddy Boy's boat. So far, a Coast Guard alert had turned up nothing. It remained as elusive as the *Mary Celeste*.

The Medical Examiner said Buddy Boy Benson had been shot with a spear gun. That didn't make sense. Buddy Boy was strictly a rod-and-reel fisherman. His charters didn't go snorkeling or use spear guns. If you wanted to go after Hogfish, or spear lobsters, he wasn't your guy. Sam Elkins would have been a better choice. The *Pretty Patty* was more of a dive boat.

Word spread along the dock that Buddy Boy Benson had been killed by pirates, blackguards who had kidnapped his charter customers and stolen the *Saint Louis Shuffle*. Sheriff Raymond scoffed at the idea; piracy was long dead, and besides no group of tourists had been reported missing.

"Besides," he said to Walter de Worcester, "there's been no kidnap demands."

Yes, Randy Ray Raymond had finally broken down and consulted Walter the Weirdo. But he was doing it on the QT. No need to let any of the *Citizen* reporters get wind of this little confab.

The sheriff had found Walter out near the old Burger King (it was now a fast-food chicken joint) on North Roosevelt. Recently, the little man had been sleeping in an alley near there, even pitched a tent. He'd been cited for trespassing, but that hasn't deterred him. Being a former lawyer, he'd defended himself by pleading "Not guilty before the Bench," pointing out that one couldn't trespass on a public roadway, even if it was a dead-end alleyway. Roads provided free access to all citizens. The judge had been sympathetic, reducing the charge to jaywalking, a $5 fine.

Now Sheriff Raymond sat with him at an outside table at Popeyes Louisiana Kitchen. A fried chicken sandwich had been Walter's price for this consultation. Recouping his $5 fine.

"Sam Elkins did it," Walter pronounced as his finished off his fries. He had demanded a combo – sandwich, fries, soft drink.

"What makes you say that?"

"Sam and Buddy Boy didn't get along. Everybody knows that. Business competitors. Buddy Boy was undercutting Sam's prices for fishing trips."

"But that's not enough to kill a man over."

"The quarrel had gotten out of hand. Last week Buddy Boy threw a bucket of fish guts onto the deck of *Pretty Patty*. Nobody saw him do it, but Sam knew who was behind the dirty deed."

"Bad blood's not enough to arrest a man over."

"Check Sam's spear guns on the boat. Bet one of them's missing the bolt."

"C'mon, you gotta give me more than that. After all, that's a Buffalo Ranch Medium Combo you're eating there."

"And it's very tasty," Walter conceded. He was an odd-looking man with thick eyeglasses and a brush moustache. He wore his usual black mourning coat and bowler hat, like a dandy who'd just stepped off the front page of the *London Times*.

"So –?"

"What cracks the case is the scene of the murder," Walter explained.

"Big Cow Key?"

"Yes," the little man nodded. "Sam Elkins owns a cabin on Big Cow Key. Likely Buddy Boy went up there to do more mischief, throw rotten fish through the window or something. Sam caught him and shot him. Probably sank the *Saint Louis Shuffle* to make you think someone killed him and stole it – the phony charter customers or pirates or some other miscreant – anybody but Sam."

"But Sam was at the dock when the *Saint Louis Shuffle* set out for the day."

"How do you know that?"

"Well, Sam said so – oh, I get it. He lied."

"Murderers often do."

"Hmm, he was trying to use a dead man as his alibi – clever."

"Righty-o."

"But there's more, right?"

"Indeed there is, my dear constable. Your deputies had rousted me from my tent in the alley, so I was sleeping on the dock. That morning Sam wasn't on his boat when Buddy Boy Benson pulled out. He told me he was going up to Big Cow Key to play a prank on ol' Sam. Guess Sam didn't think it was funny."

"How come you didn't come forward with this information?" demanded Sheriff Randall Ray Raymond. His face red as a broiled lobster.

"Because I knew you would eventually come to me. You always do."

"Well, I'll be a —"

"Now may I have my dessert? I very much like the Raspberry Cheesecake Fried Pie they serve here."

7. Meeting at Margaritaville

Barthélemy Banks

Malloy was a Key West drunk, a regular at a local watering hole known for its frozen margaritas and lost shaker of salt. He had a preferred seat at the bar, on the far end away from the window, with a good view of the stage. But Jimmy didn't perform here anymore.

As a former CIA shooter, he knew his tradecraft. Sitting in front of the large open-air window near the door was not a good idea. Old adversaries might spot him. Less of a likelihood in the dark interior of the bar hunched over a drink. Anonymity was a good thing in his line of work.

That's why he was surprised when someone called out his name. Well, his cryptonym.

"M? Is that you?"

His sector of the Central Intelligence Agency was fond of alphabet soup nomenclature. J had been his spotter. B had been his boss. With an organization known for its compartmentalization, there wasn't much call to know other names – even those of the ABC variety.

Tim Malloy didn't move. He no longer carried a gun, his hands too shaky. All he could do is sit the on the barstool and wait for the bullet to hit the base of his skull. For his own assignments, he'd preferred a behind-the-ear placement, but others in his profession went for the base of the skull or the occipital bone in the back. The human skull is composed of 22 bones in all. Behind the ear avoided that obstruction. Less chance of deflections or ricochets. Some people were literally hard-headed in his experience.

Malloy personally preferred a small handgun, a .22 like the Israeli Mossad used. Most of his fellow shooters went with a nine. Gangsters often used a .45, a large caliber that would blast through any bone – but that was ineloquent to him. He preferred a close-up shot from behind, a small report, hardly noticeable, then him fading into the crowd before anyone screamed.

He wonder what size bullet was heading his way. He didn't flinch as he said, "Yep, it's me."

"Well, I'll be danged. Fancy bumping into you here at the tail-end of the earth. I'm down here on vacation with my family."

Malloy slowly turned, recognizing the voice. It was a Company man known as K. He'd had a desk job, something administrative at Langley, accounting maybe. Malloy had met him a couple of time when he went to Headquarters for briefings. The guy had approved his expense account. Back in the day, he'd used three different credit cards with three different names, none his own.

It had been several years since M had been on the payroll. The Company had put him out to pasture. When his spotter had run away with his wife, he'd become unreliable, started to drink, lost his edge. That wouldn't do for a trained assassin. Yes, he'd once killed people for a living. But bad people, those sanctioned by the US Government as being harmful to the Greater Good.

Now, he just killed a few drinks every afternoon at Margaritaville. He didn't mind that it was a tourist dive. Hiding in plain sight at a place where no one would notice him.

Till now. An old colleague on vacation with his suburban spouse and 2.5 kids.

"Where's your wife?" smiled Malloy. Sweat trickling down the back of his neck, soaking his Tommy Bahama shirt, a decorative pattern that involved both flamingoes and bananas.

"Shopping next door at Fastbuck Freddie's. I just popped in here for a drink while she and the little ones do their damage to the family budget."

That was back before the popular department store had gone out of business, replaced on the corner of Duval and Fleming by a CVS. The world was changing around Malloy. Even an end-of-the-road town like Key West.

"What are you drinking?" asked Malloy. "It's on me."

"A mojito, thanks."

Malloy signaled to the bartender, a young guy who looked like a surfer out of an old Annette Funicello beach movie. "A schmojito," he used the slang. Similar to a margarita, the traditional Cuban highball consists of five ingredients: white rum, sugar cane juice, lime juice, soda water, and mint. Margaritas are made with Tequila as the base and triple sec as its sweetener. The mint was the big difference.

People argue over the name. Some say it's the diminutive of *mojo* ("sauce"). Others say it is an affectionate form of address for a male child or younger man, shortened from *mi hijito*. Still others claim it comes from the word *mojo*, which means "to cast a spell."

Malloy went with the latter theory, the idea that African slaves in Cuba had seen the aguardiente rum concoction as a magical potion. Mojitos and similar libations had certainly had him under a spell for several years now.

K – the visitor identified himself as Keith Heath – clinked his sweaty glass against Malloy's margarita and said "Skoal!" before taking a sip. "Hmm, this sure hits the spot on a hot day like this. Must be a hundred degrees out there on the sidewalk."

"Never been more than 95 here in Key West," corrected Malloy. "But the humidity makes it feel hotter."

"With global warming, that temperature glass ceiling may get broken," shrugged the lanky man. His blond hair was trimmed short, kind of a buzz cut. His T-shirt said DADDY'S BOY'S

DADDY. He had a three-year-old, he explained. Only one child rather than the statistical 2.5 that Malloy had imagined.

"How's B?" Malloy inquired after his old handler.

"He retired last month. Heard he moved to Colorado. Bought a ranch out there."

"Good for him. He was always a cowboy at heart."

"You were the cowboy," laughed Keith Heath. "I used to hear talk about your assignments. You were considered the renegade of the pack."

"That's long behind me. They put me out to pasture, as I'm sure you know."

"Yep, processed the severance check myself. One of my many financial duties. But as you know, nobody is ever truly severed."

"Oh?" His antenna went up. Some people would have called it his Spidey Sense.

"The new guy – C's his cryptonym – asked me to look you up while I'm down here in Key West. Has a favor to ask."

"Whoa, I'm out of it. Don't even own a gun," he lied. "My hand shakes like a palsy victim's. See?" He held out his trembling fingers as proof of his statement.

K shook his head. "No, this is not about a sanction. Nothing like that. He merely wants you to meet a Cuban who wants to turn over some of Castro's papers. You know, play go-between."

"But I'm not on the payroll, you know that as well as anyone, having processed my severance check."

"All the better. No link back to us."

"What kind of papers? Can't imagine what use Castro's papers would be."

"His diary. We want to see what he had to say about November 22, 1963."

"Kennedy's assassination?"

"Right-o. Old news, but important to know."

"Why would *El Barbuda*'s memoir matter? I thought we did it. At least that what David Atlee Phillips once told me."

"Phillips oughta know. He was knee-deep in the operation – or so I've heard."

"Then where does Castro fit in?"

"Somebody leaked the plans to Castro. He knew about it in advance. We want to know who talked."

"Why not simply ask him?"

"He won't talk to us."

"Oh, right."

"So, will you help us?"

Malloy took another sip of his drink, licking the final vestige of salt off the rim. "Why would it matter after all these years. It's been nearly six decades. Is anybody involved still alive?"

"Has to do with a name going on the wall."

"You mean those stars representing agents who died in the line of duty?"

"Yeah," nodded K. "The wall in the lobby at Langley. An accusation has been made against one of those men on the wall. The Director wants to know whether to leave it hanging or pull it off."

"And this diary will determine the truth?"

"That's what the Director believes. Who am I – a lowly pencil-pusher – to question wisdom from on high. C said he'd pay for this vacation if I could get you to handle this errand."

"So you didn't randomly bump into me." A rhetorical observation.

Keith Heath smiled. "Nothing's ever random with the Company. You know that."

"What do I get out of it? As you may recall, that severance wasn't very generous."

"True, but you were more of a liability at the time. A quick kiss-off was deemed to be the best way to handle it."

"Now here you are, hat in hand."

"No hat, just a baseball cap." He held up a cap that said CONCH REPUBLIC, the euphemism for Key West. Ol' Keith had obviously visited one of the souvenir shops that line Duval Street, storefronts that vie with the bars for dominance.

"Okay, cap. But the point is, why should I help out my former employers?"

"Money." K held up a thick packet. It had been hidden under the baseball cap. "Ten thousand very good reasons."

"That's a tidy sum for a go-fetch assignment. Must be dangerous."

"Not at all. Just a handover. You deliver the diary to me; I give you the ten."

"Why not do it yourself, keep the money. That would be a nice bonus to an accountant's salary, I'd guess."

"True. But if you don't follow orders to a tee, you wind up with someone like you – well, the former you – paying a visit. Isn't worth it."

Malloy smelled a rat. Ten grand was way too much for this kind of assignment. Maybe not, if they wanted him to kill the guy. But Keith Heath was claiming this was a clean handover of a diary. "Do I give the courier any money for his package?" he pressed.

"Got a second packet of money here." The accountant produced it for Mallory to see. "Twenty-five for him."

"You're getting a five grand vacation, I'm getting ten large ones, and the Cuban gets twenty-five – right?"

"That's right, everybody's happy."

"Okay, I'll do it," said Malloy.

So he pocketed the $25,000 for himself, gave the courier $10,000. If the man complained, he would simply say Keith Heath had shortchanged him. Let K take the heat with his bosses.

After all, that severance check *had* been rather stingy. This evened the score.

Footnote: According to the so-called diary, Fidel Castro had been meeting with an American journalist named Jean Daniel when he received word of John Fitzgerald Kennedy's death. He professed to be truly surprised. At the time, he muttered, *"Es una mala noticia."* ("This is bad news.")

Nothing startling here. Same old, same old. The $10,000 turned out to be a generous payment for the diary, in Tim Malloy's opinion. It was about as useful as a *Dick and Jane* primer.

With his $25 grand, he bought a boat.

8.

Robert Coburn

"What in the hell happened to Smokey?" Mr. Jiggs wanted to know.

"Nobody's talking," Boots told him.

"Can't have treats?" Mr. Jiggs said. "And he has a broken jaw?"

"It's a mystery."

"I could understand a bitten-off ear," said Mr. Jiggs, who happened to be missing the peak on one of his own.

The front door of the house on Angela Street, where the notice was posted, suddenly banged open and a woman stepped out.

"Shoo!" she shouted loudly and waved her hands at them. "Get away from here!"

The two cats ran across the street and hid under the stoop of a house.

The woman got into her car and drove off.

"She belongs to Smokey," Boots said.

"Not very friendly," Mr. Jiggs commented. "He could've done better, in my opinion."

"I saw a bird cage on a porch in the next block," Boots said. "Let's go have some fun."

A tiny peeping sound caught their attention as they passed a thick growth of shrubs on Passover Lane.

"Are those baby chicks I hear?" Mr. Jiggs murmured, narrowing his eyes.

Both began to slink into the bushes.

And Mr. Jiggs was right.

A mother hen with her tiny brood was busy pecking at the ground.

And that wasn't all that was there.

A large rooster stood at her side and had his fierce eyes fixed firmly on Mr. Jiggs.

Normally, a single cat would be no match for a Key West rooster but here were two young cats. That might've upped the odds in their favor except that this particular bird was none other than John Wayne.

As an aside, Key West chickens name themselves after old Hollywood movie stars according to their own personalities and ability. Not everyone is aware of that fact. But Key West cats and dogs certainly are and know to stay clear of certain individuals.

John Wayne ruffled his feathers which increased his size by twice and hurled a menacing cock-a-doodle-doo at them.

Mr. Jiggs and Boots immediately recognized who they were dealing with and choosing caution over valor, hissed and turned tail with a second more threatening cock-a-doddle-doo chasing after them.

"Phew, that was close," Boots said breathlessly, both now safely on the sidewalk at the cemetery's entrance. "I think I lost a life."

"Me, too," Mr. Jiggs said, his hair still standing on end. "That's number three. Six to go."

"What say we skip the bird cage and go to Five Brothers?" Boots suggested. "Grab a bite to eat."

Sadly, they were to be disappointed.

"You're too late," Miss Kitty told them disdainfully.

She was a purebred Persian and was quite impressed with herself. She was sunning on a bench beside the store. An empty food bowl sat beneath her on the sidewalk.

"The chickens got here first and ate everything," she said, giving them a Cheshire smile before curling up and closing her blue eyes.

"Now what?" Mr. Jiggs asked.

"There's always the Bight." Boots offered with a smile of his own.

"Bet I can beat you across the street," Mr. Jiggs challenged.

They darted into Southard Street. The oncoming car braked in time but was rear ended by the one following.

"Stupid drivers," Boots sneered, flicking his tail. "We could've been flattened. Won't they ever learn?"

They continued on without further incident until Lands End where, in an alley that ran next to a restaurant, they came upon a dead body. Even more shocking was that they knew who he was.

"It's old Ringtail Tom," Boots said. "He and Smokey were pals despite his age and ran around together."

"We should report this to the police," Mr. Jiggs said.

"There aren't any police cats," Boots shrugged. "That job is only for dogs."

"Might be risky to talk to them," Mr. Jiggs said.

"Hmm, this is curious," Boots said, his attention drawn to at oddly shaped black box near where old Tom lay.

He sniffed at a hole in the box side.

"I smell a rat," he said, swiping at it with his paw.

"Well, this *is* the waterfront," Mr. Jiggs laughed. "You'd expect plenty of them to be around. Part of the scene. Like the chickens are but then they're everywhere."

"But what is this thing?"

"Could be a special kind of food bowl the restaurant leaves for cats to keep the rats away," Mr. Jiggs said. "Like the one they put out at Five Brothers only this one's different so the chickens can't get in."

"But what about the rat?" Boots asked. "Could he get in?"

"Guess the hole's big enough," Mr. Jiggs said, crouching for a better look.

He inched inside just a little.

"Careful," Boots warned.

"Ouch!" he yelled, and quickly backed out.

"What happened? Are you all right?"

"Something made my paws tingle."

"Funny thing to happen in a food bowl," Boots said.

"Maybe that's what keeps out the rats," Mr. Jiggs said. "Rats are lower to the ground and have bare feet so they'd feel it even more."

"Makes sense to me," Boots said. "Hey, I just thought of something. Suppose Ringtail Tom and Smokey were here having a nice meal and this dirty rat shows up. He gets pissed off because they can eat there and he can't. So he picks a fight with them."

"That would explain Smokey's broken jaw," Mr. Jiggs nodded. "Cats can't take a punch there. But what happened to Ringtail Tom? No marks on him. Although he doesn't look too good."

"Wonder how many lives has he lived?" Boots pondered.

"Good question," Mr. Jiggs said. "I know he was getting up there. Maybe seven or could be eight."

"Maybe he just keeled over from all the excitement," Boots said. "Sometimes you can lose a couple of lives at once depending on the circumstances."

"I believe you've solved it, Boots."

They took a final look at Ringtail Tom and turned to leave.

"Before we go, let's have a little taste from that bowl," Mr. Jiggs said.

"Good idea," Boots agreed with a flick of his tongue.

"Looking to get your asses kicked?" a squeaky voice asked from behind them.

A huge brown rat stepped out of the shadow, dragging its tail which was as long as its body.

"Who are you?" Mr. Jiggs asked.

"I'm Biggie Rat. And you're in my alley."

"We better beat it," Books whispered nervously.

"He doesn't scare me," Mr. Jiggs whispered back with a slight tremor.

Biggie Rat chuckled.

"What's it going to be, Mr. Tough Guy?" he sneered at Mr. Jiggs.

"That's *Mr.* Jiggs to you, buster."

With an angry squeak, Biggie Rat charged. But having poor eyesight, which is common with rats, he plowed straight into the box's entrance. A cracking zap was followed by a loud squeak and then nothing more.

Days later, Mr. Jiggs and Boots were passing by Smokey's house on Angela Street. To their surprise, Smokey was sunning himself on the porch. They bounded up the steps two at a time.

"How are you doing?" Boots asked.

"On the mend," Smokey said.

"We took care of that rat who broke your jaw," Mr. Jiggs said proudly.

"Got what he deserved for scaring old Ringtail Tom to death, too," Boots added.

"What are you talking about?"

"Biggie Rat. Down at the Bight."

"I don't know any Biggie Rat and I've never been to the Bight," Smokey said. "Haven't seen Ringtail Tom in months. You say he's dead?"

"But your jaw," Mr. Jiggs said.

"Oh, that happened when I bit down too hard on a bone that was in Henry's dog dish. He lives in the house behind me. I don't see how he eats that stuff. Made me sick, too."

9. Lord Jeffrey Comes Out of Retirement – BRIEFLY

Hollis George

Lord Jeffrey Livingstone-Jones was making a tour of the colonies – at least, that's the way he thought of the Bahamas, Jamaica, and The Cayman Islands. The fact that these far-flung outposts had achieved different levels of independence didn't register with Lord Jeffrey's Anglo-centric viewpoint of the New World.

Even America was a colony-on-a-break in his mind. As the song in *Hamilton* promised, "You'll be back."

He had enjoyed his travels so far. Lord Jeffrey's son worked for British Air and got him upgraded to First Class. He had toured this corner of the British Empire in genteel comfort. The flight attendants had even served him Glenlivet in those miniature bottles. He barely remembered the flights.

On his way home – back in London he lived in a two-story Georgian in the Kensington section – he opted to stop over in Key West. He'd never been there before. But a distant relative had been stranded on the island in the late 1800s when his ship hit a reef. Some historians said the *HMS Pentacle* had been the victim of wreckers, scallywags who put up false beacons in order to salvage the cargo of cocoa coming from South America. Decedents of Simon Jones still resided in Key West.

In fact, when he phoned the residence of Richard Portnoy Jones from the airport, he got his cousin's wife. She sounded hysterical.

"My dear lady, what in the name of heaven is the matter?" asked Lord Jeffrey. He hated to encounter women in distress.

"It's Richard," came the answer in the form of a low wail. "He's been arrested for murder."

"Good Lord! Whom did he kill?" asked Lord Jeffrey. The elderly man was a retired Scotland Yard DCI, so he knew a thing or two about solving crimes. Especially murder. The highpoint of his career had been cracking the Brighton Basher case, the one where a deranged man had been hitting his victims on the head with a rubber mallet. Most died from these concussions, but one bounced back (pun intended) and identified his assailant.

"The police say Richard shot the harbor master with a flare gun. Set him ablaze like a Roman candle."

"Are you saying your husband didn't do it?"

"Of course, he didn't do it. But Chief Peterbilt says Richard's fingerprints are on the gun. My husband's going to be railroaded into prison, just because of a pig."

"A pig, did you say?" The phone connection had a lot of static.

"Petunia. She belongs to Chief Peterbilt."

"I don't see what this baconer has to do with the alleged crime."

"Last month Richard filed a complaint about Chief Peterbilt's pig with the zoning commission. People are not allowed to keep farm animals within city limits."

"The police chief's porker, you say?"

"Yes," Alice Jones sniffled. "This trumped-up charge is the chief's retribution. He was forced to move his pig to a farm in Ocala. He was upset because this small potbelly pig was a family pet, not an agricultural specimen."

"I can see he might be upset. But so much he would frame my cousin for murder?"

"Cousin?" She realized she had no idea who the stranger on the phone was. Her troubles had simply tumbled out when she answered the call.

"Distant cousins. On our fathers' side. I thought I might drop by for a family visit, but I can see I've come at a bad time."

"Richard didn't shoot Harlan Bethel with a flare gun."

"Then how did his fingerprints get on the gun?"

"Well, it *was* Richard's flare gun. He kept it in his boat. Naturally, he had handled it."

"Did your husband have any bad blood with this Bethell fellow?"

"Actually, yes. There was a disagreement over a boat slip. Harlan was going to give Richard's slip to Tiny Tom."

"Tiny Tom?"

"That's Harlan's nephew. They call Thomas Bethel that because of his diminutive size. He's a dwarf, barely four feet in height."

"And he wanted your husband's boat slip?"

"Yes, the one in front of Schooner Wharf. That's the dog bar at the Key West Bight. Tiny Tom hangs out there with his Pekinese, a nasty little mutt called Yapper. A nearby boat slip would be convenient for when Tiny Tom drinks too much. He could sleep it off in his cabin cruiser."

"Where did this murder take place?"

"On Richard's boat, *The Lady Killer*. There at the dock."

"An unfortunate name."

"No lady was killed, just the harbor master. Nearly burnt up the boat. Insurance is refusing to pay for the repairs, since Richard is accused of firing the flare gun that started the blaze."

"Can you describe the crime scene?"

"The boat's slip was at the end of the plank walkway. Nothing unusual there. It was tied securely. Directly in front of the Schooner Wharf Bar, but nobody saw a thing because Michael McCloud was performing. All eyes were on the stage."

"Nothing unusual, you say?"

"Well, one thing. The gangplank was down. Richard is a lanky, long-legged guy. He just jumps aboard, never bothers with a gangplank."

"Other than the flare gun, is there any other evidence against your husband?" By now, Lord Jeffrey was standing in the taxi line. It was a long, snaking queue comprised of vacationers with their luggage and whiny kids. He hated this part of traveling. He must remind himself to have a car waiting when he arrived back at Heathrow. Travel should be civilized, not an unruly madhouse.

"Only the blonde hair. Chief Peterbilt arrested Richard's girlfriend too."

"Girlfriend?"

"Dorothy Gildersleeve. He's been seeing her since we separated."

"Good Lord, you and your husband are living apart?"

"It's better this way. He's a terrible tomcat. The man has slept with half the women on this island. And an untold number of tourists. Not to mention his current inamorata, Dorothy Gildersleeve."

"Why arrest her?"

"A strand of her hair was found wedged in the breech of the flare gun. Proves she was there with the killer."

"Your husband, you mean?"

"Richard didn't kill anybody."

"If he didn't kill the man, why was his girlfriend present?"

"Who knows? Maybe she did it. She certainly had access to the boat where he kept the flare gun."

"If my cousin is treating you so shabbily, why do you care if he's charged with the harbor master's fiery death?"

"Because if Richard goes to jail, he won't be able to pay the child support. We have a ten-year-old son, Little Dickie. He's the island spelling bee champion."

"Congratulations to Little Dickie."

"This is all that pig's fault," she sobbed, her voice sounding distant over the phone.

"Petunia's fault?"

"Not *that* pig – Dorothy, I mean."

"How is it Dorothy Gildersleeve's fault?"

Alice Jones tried to compose herself, clearing her throat, sniffling. "You see, she is the former girlfriend of Chief Peterbilt. Left Johnny Peterbilt for my husband, that blonde tramp."

"You're saying the police chief arrested this Gildersleeve woman out of spite?"

"That – and the blonde strand of hair found stuck to the flare gun."

"Piffle. That hair can be explained."

"How so?"

"It belongs to Tiny Tom's Pekinese. You see, Tiny Tom killed his uncle in an argument over the boat slip. Harlan Bethel had changed his mind about giving it to Tiny Tom."

"How do you know that."

"You say the murder took place aboard the boat. Tiny Tom was a dwarf, too short to step aboard without the use of a gangplank. Same for his short-legged dog, a breed known for its long blonde hair."

"You'll tell this to Chief Peterbilt?"

"My word, no. But a good barrister can make the point. And Tiny Tom won't have an alibi. Your husband will have one, that Gildersleeve woman."

"But she's been arrested as an accomplice."

"Merely a lover's spat. Chief Peterbilt will drop the charges against her and your husband once he has a more viable suspect."

"Like Tiny Tom?"

"Exactly."

"How can I ever thank you?"

"No need. Family must stick together."

"Are you coming over?"

"No, I've changed my mind about this visit. Catching the next flight to New York, then jumping the pond to Jolly Old England. Too much excitement on your little island. Besides that, there are all these pigs and Pekinese – I'm not fond of animals. Allergies, you know."

10. Pink Shrimp and Pussy Power

George Davidson

The water had poor visibility, the bottom stirred up by the coming weather front. Already designated as Tropical Storm Annie, but it was likely to reach hurricane status. Coincidental that the storm had the same name as his ex-girlfriend. Her turbulent personality made it seem appropriate.

Bitch.

The wave pounded against the eroding beach. Here in Key West beaches are surprisingly few, an island with more limestone rock than sand. Higgs Beach, a favorite with tourists, was mostly artificial, the white sand barged in from the Bahamas Platform.

Dark clouds roiled in the sky, like sumo wrestlers vying for position. On the horizon he could see a large cruise ship heading out to sea, hoping to avoid being trapped by the storm. Annie was heading straight toward Key West as if aiming for a bulls-eye. Flood warnings had been issued.

Lester could see the body in the water. Like storm debris riding the waves. He was hoping it would be swept out to sea. Wouldn't do to have it tossed back on shore, as if the turbulent ocean was rejecting his gift.

A hurricane would make it look like an accidental death, the consequence of this natural disaster. FEMA volunteers would be too distracted by the devastation to worry about a stray victim.

He shouldn't be standing out here on White Street Pier in the raw wind. He could barely keep his balance. The boards were wet and slippery. If the police spotted him, they would tell him to get to the safety of a shelter. He'd have to comply.

Yes, looked like Tropical Storm Annie was going to turn into a hurricane.

Hurricanes are not as plentiful in Key West as most people think. To reach the island, those huge whirling dervishes had to cross Cuba, where the mountains broke them up, diminishing them into a tropical storm. If the hurricane veered to the left of Cuba, it missed Key West and hit New Orleans. If it went to the right of Cuba, the swirling winds swung up the Atlantic coast to strike North Carolina's Outer Banks.

The Saffir-Simpson Hurricane Scale defines hurricane strength by categories. Category 1 storms are the weakest (winds 74-95 MPH); Category 5 storms are the strongest (winds greater than 155 MPH). Typical hurricanes are about 300 miles wide. Hurricanes cause an average of 17 deaths a year.

But a tropical storm was nothing to take lightly. These rapidly rotating systems are characterized by a low-pressure center, with strong winds and heavy rain.

Thunderstorm winds cause an average of 31 deaths per year. Floods account for about 70.

Add one more for Annie.

He could see her body bobbing about in the choppy water. Why wouldn't she sink? Her lifeless form seemed to have a natural buoyancy, like an air-filled float in a swimming pool. Maybe he should have wrapped her in chains or tied an anchor around her ankles.

He'd do it better next time.

If ever there was a next time.

Lester had not meant to hit Annie, but she'd made him so angry, accusing him of infidelity. Okay, so it was true. But Dorotka meant nothing to him, just a quick fling. Too bad Dorotka had a big mouth, bragging about her night with him. If she'd kept her trap shut, Annie would have never known.

Annie and Dorotka worked at the same club, Bubba's Boobies & Booties. Both of them were pole dancers, a common profession for Czechs. The two women were slender blondes, could've passed for sisters.

Annie's name was actually Annya Adamec. She danced under the stage name of "Champagne." Dorotka Blahnik was known at the club as "Perignon."

Dorotka might be a threat. She had an agile mind for a drug-addled stripper. She would put two and two together, once she realized Annie was missing. She knew he had an unchecked temper. And that Annie had figured out that he and Dorotka had hooked up last week.

Would she go to the police?

Probably.

That meant Dorotka would have to go too. Maybe another "casualty of the storm."

Lester stood there at the end of the pier, braving the strong wind, watching the dark ocean move in mysterious ways. Eventually, the body disappeared beneath the water. Or maybe the rain was too heavy for him to see that far. Nothing more to do here. May as well go back to the apartment building and take care of that big-mouthed Dorotka.

Many of the Czechoslovakian strippers lived in the same building, their rent subsidized by Bohuchval, the handler who managed all the strippers for the club. He rotated them between Prague and Key West like a revolving door. The girls came over on a Green Card, sent money home, and after three months returned to Czechoslovakia to apply for a new visa. They repeated the process over and over. Stripping in America paid much better than working as a sales clerk in Liberec or Ostrava.

Bohuchval – better known as Bo to his friends – was an Incredible Hulk kind of a guy, maybe 6-foot-4 and weighing in at 300 pounds. He would have made a good bouncer if he hadn't preferred managing his "flock of chickens." He was very protective of the girls; they produced a steady income for him.

Some of them, Bo rented out as escorts (wink, wink). Lester didn't mind Annie taking an occasional assignment. The money was good. So why should she be so jealous over his dalliance with Dorotka? Tit for tat, he'd told her.

That's when she lost it.

And he hit her.

Now he'd have to hook up with another of Bo's flock. He was used to being a kept man, living off the earning of a girlfriend. Fortunately for him, Annie had been orphaned last year when her parents died in an automobile accident back in Prague. Being an only child, she had no one to send money home to. That allowed Lester to live in style.

Dorotka didn't have a boyfriend. Most of her earnings went to a younger sister back in Czechoslovakia. No matter, she'd be dead within an hour or two.

Talkative bitch.

Bo was in the lobby when he got there. Blue Water Manor was more of a flea trap than a manor. The rooms were small. Bathrooms were shared, not an ideal situation for showgirls who spent several hours in front of a mirror applying makeup. Most of them "put on their face" at the club. Bubba's Boobies & Booties had a very large dressing room.

"Hey, Lester," the big handler greeted him. "You seen Annya? Don't like her being out in this storm. Gonna get worse, likely turn into a 'cane.'"

"Nope, thought she'd be here," he lied.

"Ain't seen her all afternoon. Club's closed for the next few days. This storm's gonna be a bad one."

"Dorotka here?"

"Up in her room. Nailing plywood over her window."

The town was pretty well boarded up by now. Home Depot was out of plywood, but Bo had scored some from a contractor he knew. It wasn't his job to take care of the Blue Water apartment building, but 13 of his chickens lived here in these cramped quarters, so he was merely protecting his investment.

Lester trounced up the stairs to the second floor. Dorotka's tiny room was on the northwest corner, the safest side from a hurricane traveling from the south. He didn't bother to knock on the door, merely flung it open and advanced on her with deadly purpose.

She turned from the window where she'd been nailing a slab of plywood. "Lester, what are you doing here. I thought you were out looking for Annya."

"Annie's dead. And you're gonna join her."

"W-what?"

"I had to kill her. And you're next." He reached for her neck, fingers pressing into the pliant flesh, squeezing.

Whak!

The blonde hit him on the side of the head with the hammer in her hand. He fell like a heifer in a stockyard slaughter house.

Bo appeared at the door. "You all right?" he shouted. He looked worried.

Dorotka cleared her throat. "Y-yes. But I think I just killed Lester."

"No big loss. He was a parasite, that *grázl*."

"He said he killed Annya and was going to kill me too."

"That's why I came up to check on you. He had blood on his shirt sleeve. I figured he'd done something bad."

"Poor Annya."

"Yeah, she was one of my biggest earners. I'm going to miss that *děvka*."

"What about Lester." She looked down at the dead body.

"I'll take him down and dump him off the White Street Pier. If he washes ashore, he'll be counted as a casualty of the storm."

"Good idea. I don't want to explain him to the police. And White Street Pier is a good place to dump him. Annya always loved it down there."

"When I get back, we can have some pink shrimp with beer and ride out the storm. I got a take-out order from the Half Shell Raw Bar just before they closed down for the storm." He pinched her on the butt to show his affection.

"Bohuchval —" she admonished.

"Annya was good," he said, "but you was always my favorite."

Dorotka grinned. "Forget the shrimp," she said to him. "Get rid of the body and I'll fuck your brains out."

11. Brains Matter/
Brain Matter

Jack Mazur

Jacques had bought a convenience store at the corner of Caroline and William's Streets. The first Anglo Saxon to own the place in thirty years. He knew that there could be problems. Multitudes of homeless and drug-addled hung outside by the front door. Shoplifting was a local hobby. Robbery wasn't unheard of.

From the very first Jacques had a plan. When he initially bought the store he padded the wall opposite the register with two Serta mattresses, some pillows and an inch thick blanket of rubber mat. This was all covered by an artistically designed curtain that featured fish, boats and girls in bikinis. Everything else was just stocked store shelves with a continuing give and take. Sell and re-stock. Customers coming and customers going.

One day two lowlifes came in to rob him. One smelly middle-aged shirtless man and one mostly toothless female with greasy hair that looked like rope. Old rope. The worst kind. The shirtless man stuck a gun in Jacques face and demanded the money. Can't say Jacques was aghast. This instant had been coming for months.

"Gimme the money," said the shirtless guy.

"Get to it," said the old piece of rope.

"Sure thing," said Jacques, "I'm all over it."

The robbers were not aware that Jacques had pressed a button with his foot that notified the local police concerning his situation. He was as cool as a stork on a German rooftop! "Hey," he said, "I've got a surprise." A panel behind his head moved from left to right. When it was full opened one could see what looked like a small cannon pointed towards the customer desk. Head level. It was, in fact, a harbor cannon. One of those gadgets used in the 1700-1800s that would fire to let anchored boats know that now there was dock space so they could unload their cargo. Gunpowder charge. No ammo.

These guns had no rifling. There was no need to load it with anything. It was a signal gun and no more. Until Jacques got a hold of it. It was full of powder with a lot of broken metal kitchen implements inside. It had a serious attitude. "Still wanna rob me?" asked Jacques. The two losers decided to get aggressive. The shirtless guy started swinging his gun at Jacques. The rope woman started singing out curses. Jimmy Buffett was playing on the radio. Jacques stepped on another button.

The harbor cannon spit out its vitriol consisting of a six-piece place setting for a dinner of that many. The Serta mattresses, pillows and rubber matting held two separate heads. The robbery attempt was essentially ended. Just then the police showed up.

Florida has a Stand Your Ground law. Jacques was in a bit of trouble for going over the line but in the end, hey, he was getting robbed. They made him get rid of the cannon. The defeated and dead robbers were buried in paupers graves in Miami. Jacques paid for the transport.

When Jacques re-sold the store a few years later he showed the new owner the panel behind the register and how to re-load his newly acquired Gatlin gun.

12. Conched Out

William Bahlke

PART ONE

Mohammad Owadad followed the shoreline, gripping the roots of the mangrove trees to steady himself, sinking deeper and deeper into the muck with each step. Sweat poured from his brow. He paused and studied his left hand. In it, the white panties he'd kept as a souvenir were now beet red, soaked with his blood. Saltwater invaded his wound, the pain shot up his arm and into his chest, stealing his concentration. He shook it off, readjusted his heavy backpack, and squinted toward the darkness ahead of him. Over his shoulder the lights of Key West were aglow. He turned and punched his fist in the air. *"Marg bar Âmrikâ!* Death to America!"

Mohammad continued his trek, undetected by the cars and trucks speeding along US 1, the Overseas Highway. Through the branches, he could see the headlights of the vehicles as they passed over the bridge spanning the Boca Chica Channel, four lanes and a half-mile long, a bridge Mohammad knew well. Thinking about it brought a smile to his face.

He walked on, reaching the skiff he had tied up and camouflaged five days earlier. With his good hand, he pulled away branches and fronds and lowered his backpack to the floor of the boat. The moon peeked through the dark clouds, lighting up the night sky. He dropped the panties beside the backpack and looked once again at his injured hand. He would probably lose the finger, a small price to pay for a mission complete, a job well done. "Praise Allah!"

Mohammad checked his watch. The intercept at the channel marker was still an hour away. He had time. He reached into his backpack and pulled out a T-shirt he'd purchased along Duval Street. He'd worn it in a failed attempt to fit in as a tourist. He pulled the Bowie knife from its sheath on his belt and studied it, streaked with blood, but not his blood. He swished the knife in the Gulf water and used it to slice off a strip of cloth from the T-shirt. He wrapped his injured hand and with his teeth, helped secure a knot.

From the backpack, he pulled a bottle of bourbon and a cigar, forbidden at home where he would arrive in two days to a hero's welcome. Sitting on the edge of the skiff, he lit the cigar and took a swig of whiskey. He studied the sky where dark clouds had once again smothered the moonlight. The wind suddenly shifted, picking up speed, and bringing in cool, refreshing, moist air, signs of a coming storm and from what he'd read, a bad one. "Praise Allah!"

~ ~ ~

The bar fight had not been part of the plan. The man and his whore had been sitting near the door at Don's Place when Mohammad walked in. The man was as big as a bear, full of tattoos, and wore a leather vest on a ninety-degree September night.

"Here comes a raghead!" he'd barked loud enough for all to hear. "He's got a small one. They all do." The whore laughed and made a one-inch gesture with her fingers.

The fight spilled out of the bar, into the parking lot, and then to the dark corner behind The Old Town Fitness. The onlookers kept their distance, chanting, cheering, egging them on. The big man was quick to pull his knife, slashing wildly and slicing into Mohammad's outreached hand. But Mohammad's knife was bigger, and he was the better fighter. The whore was on Mohammad's back kicking and screaming as the Bowie ripped the big man from belly to chest. Mohammad rolled the whore off his back and pressed the knife to her throat. He jacked up her skirt, ripped off her white panties, and pinned her legs with his knees. Pulling himself out of his pants, he growled, "I'm bigger than you've ever had, whore!"

He hadn't killed her because he'd seen in her eyes how much she wanted to die.

~ ~ ~

Mohammad took one last drag and tossed the cigar and the bottle into the water. He slid the skiff from the shoreline, climbed in, and yanked the outboard's pull cord twice, starting it up. He headed east, navigating from memory at first, before seeing a flash of light in the distance, three blinks, a pause, and then two more, the signal. He followed the flashing light until he reached the speedboat with its engine idling, adrift by the channel marker.

Mohammad stood and waved. The man on the powerboat did not respond. What was in his hand? There was a loud pop and then another. Mohammad clenched his chest, winced in pain, and dropped to his knees, He looked up at the now smiling man and then down at the bloody panties. "Praise All . . . ah!"

PART TWO

Miss McConnell's Third Grade Class
Career Day

"Good morning, class. My name is Robert Turner. I'm an engineer with the City of Key West."

A small voice rang out, "My dad's in charge of the whole town."

I looked down at my son, Robbie, sitting in the front row sporting a big smile. For the occasion, he'd worn his Sunday best. He'd spent an hour shining his shoes, taking extra care in the bathroom, making sure he parted his hair just right. He had on the glasses he picked out because, as he'd put it, "They make me look older." He had the slide rule my father had given me sitting on his desk for all to see. I'd taught Robbie a few tricks with it, and he was hoping to show off to his classmates later in the day.

"Thank you, son." I shook my head. "But I think the mayor might take exception to that."

My gaze drifted to Miss McConnell, Sara, standing in the back of the room. She winked and smiled. Our eyes locked. I smiled back.

"What does an engineer do?"

A little blonde girl stood by her desk in the second row. I suddenly realized that the hours I'd spent preparing my presentation had been a waste of time. I glanced at the little girl's nametag.

"Well, Amy, an engineer does a lot of different things. We make sure your roads and bridges are safe for cars and bicycles. We design and maintain the pipes that bring clean water to your house and the pipes that carry dirty water away. We watch over the power lines that bring you electricity and…"

"Where does our drinking water come from?" A little boy, Gary, waved his hand and squirmed in his seat.

I caught Sara smiling again. I'd lost total control, and we both knew it. Robbie's hand shot up.

"Yes, son. Do you want to answer Gary's question?" Robbie stood, faced the class, and cleared his throat.

"Most of our water comes all the way from the mainland in a huge pipe. Robbie made a big circle with his arms. That's where our electricity comes from too, in those big power lines you see along the highway." Robbie turned and sat down. I knew the smile. He was proud of himself. I'm proud of him too.

~ ~ ~

I call him my little man. When he was just three days old, the ride home from the hospital had been just the two of us. The funeral had been a week later. I will love his mother, Katherine, forever. I've created a special place for us, a bench in the clouds where we meet and talk. Recently, she told me it was time for me to move on. I told her I would never give up my seat on the bench. She said I didn't have to, that there was plenty of room. I'd give anything to hold her just one more time. She was my soul mate, and she gave me a special gift. Robbie and I are best friends, inseparable.

~ ~ ~

I was about to call on Jamie in the back of the room when the lights in the classroom flickered. Seconds later my cell phone vibrated on the desk. The text was from Mandy Thomas, Special Assistant to the Mayor.

"Robert, we have a situation. He needs you here ASAP. Please hurry!"

PART THREE

I'd been in the mayor's conference room a number of times but never for a meeting quite like this one. In the back of the room, an obviously upset Bob Landers, the president of the Chamber of Commerce, had the police chief cornered. Marty Stillwell, the top dog at our local National Weather Service office, was on his cell phone, shaking his head, and rubbing his temples. Two men from the Coast Guard, whom I'd never met, sat at attention, their eyes focused on a red folder on the table in front of them. The undersheriff from the Monroe County Sheriff's Department stood off to the side, stirring his coffee, and eyeing a full box of donuts. I noted that the city manager was not in attendance. I would later learn that he was out of town attending his sister's funeral.

The projection screen in the front of the room was down, and Mandy Thomas was pecking away at her laptop in anticipation of the mayor's arrival. I took a seat along the wall. Mandy glanced over with a half-smile and a head nod.

"Good morning, gentlemen." The mayor had come in through a side door. "Let's get started." His welcoming smile quickly turned all business, as he took his place at the head of the table. Those who were standing scrambled for a seat.

The mayor turned to his right. "Marty, let's start with you. What's the latest on the hurricane? Still headed west?"

Marty Stillwell placed his phone on the table and took a deep breath. "To tell you the truth, Mayor, we just don't know at this point."

"What's that?" The mayor coughed three times, excused himself with an index finger, and pulled a handkerchief from his pants pocket. He wiped his mouth and with his left hand gave Marty the "go ahead" signal.

Marty shifted in his seat. "We do know she's a Category One, sitting stationary southeast of Cuba, and getting stronger every update. The spaghetti models are all over the place. This weather pattern, it's like nothing we've seen before. There's a strong high to our east and a front trying to make its way south. The steering currents are weak, and the water temps in the Gulf are at record highs. We're keeping a close eye on her. If she heads our way, it could happen fast, sixty hours, maybe less. I'll know more after the eleven o'clock."

"Jesus Christ!" The mayor shot Marty a look. "With all that fancy equipment over there that's the best you can do? How in the hell are we supposed to . . .?" Beads of sweat spotted the mayor's face. He took a deep breath and exhaled. "Sorry, Marty, I'm a little under the weather, no pun intended. Anyway, if anyone spots Jim Cantore on the island, how 'bout giving me a heads up." There was a moment of nervous laughter around the table. "I guess we'll just wait for the eleven o'clock to –"

"With all due respect, Mr. Mayor." The police chief interrupted. "We need to get the tourists out of here now, clear the roads, and prepare for a full evacuation." The undersheriff nodded in agreement. The chief continued, "We've got two cruise ships scheduled in port tomorrow. They should be rerouted, pronto. And the tour buses from Miami, they need to be –"

Bob Landers jumped to his feet. "Come on, Chief, that's overkill, and it's bad for business. You heard the man, it's just a Cat One, and we have no idea where it's going. For all we know, the damn thing's heading to New Orleans. That poor city's got a bull's eye on its welcome sign."

"Gentlemen! Gentlemen!" The mayor used his handkerchief to wipe his brow. He looked at his watch. "It's nine fifteen. We'll wait for the eleven o'clock. Now, let's get an update from the Coast Guard. Wait a minute." He scanned the room. "Where's my engineer?" He spotted me and smiled. "There you are, Robert. Come join us. I want you in on this." He motioned me over.

I moved to the table and took a seat next to Mandy. The taller of the two men dressed in blue stood up and opened the red folder.

"Mr. Mayor, as you know, today at 0800 we located an abandoned skiff adrift in Hawk Channel, not unusual for Key West, I know. But this one had been wiped clean with a solvent, and someone did a lousy job trying to sink it. Upon closer inspection, we discovered what appeared to be bloodstains on the engine's throttle. The cleaning crew must have missed that." The Guardsman paused and gave the mayor a half smile. "We towed it in and ran some tests. It was blood all right, human blood. On top of that, we found traces of gunpowder in the bait well."

"Gunpowder? Are you sure?" The mayor's voice seemed to trail off. Up close, I could see that his eyes were glazed over, and his skin was taking on a grayish tint.

"We're sure, Mr. Mayor. Our K-9, Sparky, did three tours in Iraq. She knows gunpowder when she smells it, that's for sure." He smiled again. "That's my report, sir."

The mayor looked up. "Sheriff, your men on top of this?"

The sheriff stood up, walked over, and dimmed the conference room lights. "We're all over it, sir." He nodded to Mandy who tapped a few times on her laptop. An image of a man, obviously Middle Eastern, appeared on the projection screen.

The sheriff pulled a laser pointer from his shirt pocket. "Here's a picture of our suspect from last night's stabbing and rape. We got this off the security camera inside the liquor store at Don's Place."

"Wait a minute." The mayor interrupted, "Are you saying that last night's murder and this mystery skiff are somehow related? That doesn't make sense."

"Hear me out, sir, please." The sheriff gave Mandy a nod, and a second image appeared on the screen. "Here's our suspect at nine forty-five buying a fifth of Jack Daniels." Mandy tapped again. "He exits the store and walks into the bar next door. Eyewitnesses claim that he set a package on the bar and immediately went after one of the patrons. You all know the rest of that story. The amazing thing is that he had the balls to come back into the bar after the fight to retrieve the bottle. We missed him by two minutes. He's still at large. We're testing several blood samples recovered at the scene. We should have preliminary results by this afternoon."

"I'm sorry, Sheriff, but you've lost me." The mayor scratched his head. "I don't see how these two things are . . ."

"Here's the thing, sir." A new picture appeared on the screen. "My men were searching the shoreline this morning near the Boca Chica Bridge landward from where the skiff was recovered. They found this, a half-empty fifth of Jack Daniels. It may be a coincidence, but we're running it through the lab for prints and DNA."

The mayor shook his head. "I'll be damned. Good work, Sheriff. Now, I've gotta go lie down for a few minutes. I'll see everyone back here at eleven, sharp. Thank you, gentlemen. You too, Mandy."

~ ~ ~

Minutes later, I was in my city-issued Ford Explorer headed out of town on US 1. Sitting in the passenger seat next to me was Darrell Jackson, an engineering intern in his senior year at the University of Florida. At six foot ten, Darrell was all arms and legs. In addition to being an excellent student, he was one hell of a basketball player and a starter for the Gators.

"Where we headed, boss?"

I looked over and smiled. He knew I didn't like being called that, but it seemed he couldn't help himself, boss or sir, never Robert like I'd asked.

"There's something up ahead I want to check out," I said, and went on to brief Darrell on that morning's meeting. He listened carefully.

"They use gunpowder to make bombs. You're worried about the bridge, aren't you, boss?"

I grimaced. "Better safe than sorry. Now listen, we're almost there. We'll cross over the bridge and work our way back on foot. Grab those orange vests from the back seat. I'll get the extension mirror from the trunk when we get out."

I spotted the bridge up ahead. My stomach did a somersault as I remembered a story my dad had once told me.

He had served as a Lieutenant Colonel for the 1st Infantry Division in Vietnam. He'd said that in retreat his men would often dynamite bridges to slow down the advancing enemy. "The Cong would rebuild 'em, and we'd blow 'em up again, blow 'em to smithereens," he'd bragged.

I shook off the memory, slowed down, and pulled into the right lane behind a large dump truck. With a forty-ton capacity, it was hauling what appeared to be a full load of clean fill dirt. It's commonplace to see this type of material arriving in Key West from up the Keys or even the mainland, but in all my time here, I'd never seen clean fill dirt heading north. I made a mental note of the truck's tag number.

As we approached the arch of the bridge, the truck veered to its left, straddling the two northbound lanes. It slowed to a crawl and then stopped. The driver jumped from the cab, dashed in front of the truck, climbed onto the concrete barrier, and leaped into the water twenty feet below.

"Shit! Did you see that?" Darrell's eyes blinked rapidly. "And look over there." He pointed across the barrier to the southbound lanes where a similar truck had come to a stop, blocking traffic

My heart pounded in my chest. "Darrell, listen up! We've got to clear the bridge. Take the southbound lanes." I pointed forward. "Do whatever it takes. Get people out of their cars and off this bridge. Go! Go!"

Before I could unbuckle my seatbelt, open the door, and grab my cell phone, Darrell was out of the vehicle working his way along the concrete barrier. He had removed his shirt and was waving it frantically at the confused drivers. Luckily, a deputy was second in line behind the dump truck. He saw the intensity on Darrell's face and took immediate action.

I climbed out and ran between stopped cars, screaming at the top of my lungs. It was the only time in my life I wished I'd had a badge. After a minute, I looked back. People had gotten out of their cars and were following me. It was working.

I stopped long enough to help a mother free her infant from his car seat. "Run! Run!" An elderly man struggled to his feet and staggered. I put my arm around him, helped him along for a few steps, and then sent him ahead.

I was getting close to land when a blast launched me skyward, suspending me in slow motion. Chucks of concrete flew past me. My skin felt like it was on fire. The explosion echoed in my ears. I couldn't breathe. I couldn't think. When I finally landed, I bounced along the asphalt for what seemed like forever. I rolled to a stop, curled into a ball, and blacked out.

When I came to, my face and arms were bloody. I stood up. Several people were lying on the pavement in front of me, but a large group was standing at the edge of the bridge. I turned around. A huge span of the bridge was gone. Several power poles had snapped like toothpicks, and sparks were flying everywhere. I struggled to my feet and limped toward the crowd, helping people up along the way.

I looked back again, hoping that Darrell and the people on the other side of the bridge were safe. I walked down the embankment to get a closer look. Water was spewing from the fractured water main. The northern landmass seemed so far away. I thought of my dad. For the first time in my life, I knew what it was like to be at war. That's when it hit me. Key West was an island again, all to itself, cut off from the mainland for the first time in over ninety years.

PART FOUR

After being treated by the paramedics and giving my statement to the police, I made three calls. The first was to Sara.

"Hey, it's me."

"Oh, my God! Robert! Are you okay? This thing, it's all over the Internet. Somebody posted that an engineer was¾" Her voice softened to a whisper, "Was killed. I've been so worried. I left messages. Where are you?"

"I'm still at the bridge. I'm fine, just a few cuts and bruises. I'm about to catch a ride back to City Hall, but I wanted to check on you and Robbie. Would you mind taking him home with you after school? I might be awhile."

"We're already here. We're all right. We're playing Monopoly."

"I'm the banker." I heard Robbie in the background.

"They sent everyone home." Sara's voice shook. "Schools are closed until further notice. Parents picking up their kids were hysterical. This is crazy! What's going on, Robert?"

"I don't know for sure, but it's not good. Stay inside, please, and conserve your batteries. There won't be electricity for a while. If you still have water pressure, fill the tub, but don't drink out of the tap. I gotta go. I'll call you in a bit. You gonna be okay?"

She whispered again, "Robert, I'm scared."

"I gotta admit, I'm a little scared myself." I winced, feeling the pain in my right shoulder getting worse. "But we'll get through this, I promise."

"Robert?"

"Yes?"

"I . . . I . . ." She paused. "Just be careful, please!"

~ ~ ~

I'd met Sara in June outside Sandy's Café on White Street. We had both ordered large coffees to go, hers with cream, mine black. They had mixed up the order. After exchanging cups, I had asked where she was from, a standard question on an island where on any given day the tourists can outnumber the locals, sometimes four to one. "I live here now," she'd answered. "I moved from Tampa about a month ago. I'm a teacher. I start at Gerald Adams Elementary in the fall. How about you? From around here?"

I don't remember my answer. I do remember her beautiful hazel eyes and her sweet smile. I remember the next morning and the next and the next, sitting in Bayview Park, sipping coffee, and talking. I remember the first time she took my hand and thanked me for being such a good friend. I remember walking Robbie into his classroom on the first day of the new school year and seeing her in the front of the room. My heart pounded when I introduced my little man to his new teacher, Miss McConnell.

~ ~ ~

My second call was to Mandy Thomas who gave me a bucket full of bad news. In addition to the bridge, explosive devices had damaged the electrical substation on Big Coppitt Key, several water storage tanks around town, and the generators at the sewage treatment plant. No water, no sewer, no electricity, no escape, a logistical nightmare.

Mandy went on to say that the FBI had flown in agents from Miami who would be handling the investigation. The governor had declared a state of emergency, and National Guard troops were on their way to help patrol the streets and keep the peace.

"And, Robert," Mandy's voice cracked, "the mayor . . . He's been rushed to the hospital. His heart. He just can't catch a break.

He was conscious, and he should be all right, but he's pissed, and he's worried about the town." She paused. "He brought up your name, said that you've been around a long time, that you know this town as well as anyone. He trusts you, Robert." Her tone softened. "He's put you in charge. I've drawn up an executive order. Hurry back here, will you?"

My third call was to the Naval Air Station's commanding officer, Captain Sean McSweeney. He didn't answer his cell, so I left a detailed message.

~ ~ ~

Katherine and I had met the captain and his wife years ago at a community fundraiser. The four of us hit it off, and we'd started going out to dinner together on a regular basis. Sean and I became tennis buddies, playing on Saturday afternoons. Monday night was poker night, where I was often his guest on the base.

When Katherine died, Sean came to my rescue. I'm not sure what I would have done without him. He's someone I can talk to, someone I can rely on. Robbie calls him Uncle Sean. I call him my best friend.

~ ~ ~

On the ride back to town in a patrol car, I heard on the scanner that the folks on the north side of the bridge were all going to be okay. Several of them had been treated at the scene. Three had been transported to the hospital in Marathon, but none of their injuries were life threatening.

As we turned onto Flagler Avenue, I saw that the street was lined with people. They had come out of their houses and were standing in their front yards acting anxious and confused, pacing and shaking their heads. I saw a lady on her knees crying, her hands pressed together in prayer.

Lines at the gas stations were backed up around the block. Drivers honked their horns and cursed at the people in front of them. Traffic lights were out, and cars were inching along. Patience was already running thin.

I cracked the window and listened to a cacophony of sirens blaring in the distance. My driver showed no reaction to the commotion. The officer hadn't said a word the entire trip. He seemed fidgety and anxious to drop me off, seemingly ready to return to his regular duties, probably wondering what he would find when he did.

As we passed the high school, I checked my messages. The first three were from Sara. The last was from Marty Stillwell. His call had come in a little after eleven.

"Robert, it's Marty. Mandy asked me to call you with the latest on Hurricane Cindy. "She's a Cat Three, heading north. She's found a seam. between the pressure systems and is expected to move our way at a pretty good clip. It's safe to assume that we're in for a rough ride. We could experience hurricane force winds within forty-eight hours, maybe sooner. I'll call you after the next advisory. And, Robert, good luck."

I thanked the officer for the ride and walked into City Hall. The lobby was overflowing with the town's employees. I heard someone shout, "He's here!" The room grew silent. Everyone turned and faced me. I glanced around at my friends and colleagues, some of whom I'd known for many years. In all of their eyes, I could see the same question. "What now?"

PART FIVE

I got along with just about everyone. One notable exception was the deputy chief of police, Captain Bradley Snell, who had just stormed into my office and slammed the door.

I looked up and took a deep breath. "Good afternoon, Captain. Thanks for coming. Have a seat."

"I'll stand. What do you want?" He reeked of Old Spice.

Mandy, who had been sitting across from me taking notes, rolled her eyes and closed her laptop.

The captain stared me down, his face a chiseled mask. I broke his glare and shook my head. There was something about this man that made my skin crawl. Just being in the same room with him was like an unplanned trip to the principal's office. He was a bully's bully, and I couldn't help but wonder why he still wore a belt full of bad boy tools. His three-piece suit looked ridiculous donned with a Taser gun, pepper spray, and a pistol.

I glanced at Mandy and then back at the captain, locking eyes. "Captain, I wanted to talk to you about the Police Department's plan to evacuate the island, first the tourists and then those locals who choose to leave." His brow creased. I lowered my head and rubbed my temples. "Please tell me you have a plan, Captain." Without looking up, I could feel his daggers.

"Evacuate the island? Just how we supposed to do that, Mister Engineer? Some Muzzy blew up the Boca Chica. Or did you forget that minor detail? We gonna hand out snorkels and have 'em all swim to Miami?" He turned and took a step toward the door.

My jaw tightened. "Have a seat, Captain, or I'll report your refusal to cooperate with the mayor's office during a time of crisis

86

to the appropriate state and federal authorities, as well as your boss."

He studied my demeanor and barked, "I don't have all day. Get to the point." He slowly sat down.

My phone vibrated. I held up my index finger and read a text from Sean McSweeney.

I let out a deep breath. "Okay, Captain, here's *my* plan. The Navy has fourteen vehicle transport barges. Each barge can carry up to twenty cars. We'll load up the tourists at a makeshift ramp at the Truman Waterfront and unload them at the base on Boca Chica. If all goes well, we'll have 'em all out of here in –" I did a quick calculation in my head. "Thirty-six hours. We'll work on the locals after that, if there's time before the storm."

I nodded at Mandy who opened her laptop. She cleared her throat and read from the screen. "Airlines are bringing in extra planes to evacuate their ticketed customers and to accommodate others who may want a flight off the island. Cruise ships have been ordered out of port, and future dockings have been suspended. The Monroe County Sherriff's Department has initiated a mandatory evacuation for the upper Keys, clearing US 1 in anticipation of our boatlift evacuation plan. We have arranged for nautical shipments of bottled water, canned goods, toilet paper, batteries and ice, as well as kitty litter.

"Kitty litter?" Snell interrupted, "Why the hell do we need kitty litter?"

Mandy ignored him and continued, "Gasoline sales have been restricted to a five-gallon per person maximum, reserving fuel for essential vehicles and power generators. And lastly, several boatloads of Port-A-Johns will be delivered shortly after the storm passes." Mandy closed her laptop and glanced over at Snell.

He shot her a condescending look. "Okay, why the kitty litter?"

Mandy gave me a quick wink. I took the hint. "Well, Captain, it's to help clear the stench when people like you take a crap and have no way to flush. I'll send over a couple extra bags with your name on 'em. Now, regarding my plan, I'm counting on your department's full cooperation. You're free to go."

~ ~ ~

There would be no time to evacuate the locals.

The next afternoon, while meeting with two FBI field agents, I was given the five o'clock advisory. Hurricane Cindy's winds had reached 135 miles per hour. The storm's barometric pressure was dropping rapidly. She was headed north and picking up speed. Key West was in the cone, and there was growing concern that the island could suffer a direct hit.

In the meeting, the agents had reported that ISIS had claimed responsibility for the bombings. That, the agents had said, was good news. "ISIS never claims responsibility until after a particular mission is complete. Chances are they're done here." Somehow, driving down Duval Street an hour later, seeing panicked looks on the faces of folks boarding up their businesses, I didn't feel very good about the FBI's "good news."

Darrell Jackson, who had remained at the Boca Chica Bridge to assist the Corp of Engineers and the Department of Transportation with their initial damage assessment, was back in Key West and sitting in the passenger seat next to me.

"Damn, boss, a little thing like a Cat Four storm sure hasn't stopped the party." He pointed to a crowd standing on the sidewalk outside of Sloppy Joe's drinking beer and having fun. I rubbed my eyes, looked at their smiling faces, and let out a deep sigh. I was going on thirty hours with no sleep. I wasn't sure which sounded better, a soft pillow or a stiff drink.

Sloppy's and a few other bars had remained open, operating on generated power and using up what was left of their ice supply. They had pledged to stay open 24/7 during the storm, no matter what. The police chief was about to spoil their plans. A curfew would be announced within a few hours. Being out on the streets was just too dangerous. People would be urged to ride out the storm in the relative safety of their homes or at one of the island's two official shelters. I'd never cared for the expression "hunker down," but that's exactly what we were about to do.

After another loop around the island, I dropped Darrell off at his apartment on Angela Street and wished him well. I was anxious to get to Sara's to help her with final preparations and to see Robbie.

I had left Mandy to button up City Hall. All nonessential employees had been sent home to be with their families. We had worked around the clock. There was nothing left to do. Now, it was time to wait and watch. What might turn out to be the most devastating hurricane in Key West's history was just over a hundred miles away and bearing down on us. I rounded the corner onto Eaton Street, pulled into a parking space in front of the Key West United Methodist Church, closed my eyes, and said a prayer.

PART SIX

The *Key West Post, September 23, 2017, 6:30 p.m.* – **City Hall announces the successful evacuation of approximately seventeen thousand tourists.** The boatlift operation has been suspended.

In other news, the city has called on residents living in flood prone areas (areas that flooded during Hurricane Wilma) to seek shelter with friends and relatives residing in structures at higher elevations.

Vehicles parked in flood prone areas should be moved to higher ground. The Parking Department has arranged for free parking in all public and private parking garages on the island. Spaces are still available for several hundred vehicles on a first come, first serve basis. Shuttle services are being provided.

The Key West Post, September 23, 2017, 8:00 p.m. – **Several businesses robbed on Duval Street.** The Key West Police Department has confirmed that two jewelry stores and a liquor store each located on Duval Street were robbed early this evening. The perpetrators are still at large.

The Key West Post, September 23, 2017, 9:10 p.m. – **Mayor is reportedly doing fine.** Mayor Davis was medevacked to Miami's Jackson Memorial Hospital yesterday and is recovering in the ICU following a successful quadruple bypass surgery. A family spokesman reported, "The mayor is awake, alert, and is expected to make a full recovery."

The Key West Post, September 23, 2017, 10:30 p.m. – **Police Chief mandates curfew. The Mayor's office calls for calm in advance of the approaching storm.** Acting mayor, Robert Turner, issued a statement urging all citizens to obey the police chief's thirty-six-hour curfew and to remain indoors during the storm event. He emphasized, "Please don't risk the lives of our emergency personnel by breaking the rules."

National Weather Service, Miami, September 23, 2017, 11:00 p.m. – **Hurricane Cindy continues to move north-northwest at 8 mph.** The Category Five storm, with sustained wind speeds of 160 mph, is now the strongest Atlantic cyclone since 2007's Hurricane Felix. It is still too early to predict exactly when and where landfall will occur. A hurricane warning is now in effect for the Florida Keys, northward to Miami and Fort Lauderdale on the east coast, and Naples and Fort Myers on the west coast. The balance of Florida remains under a hurricane watch.

The Miami Journal, September 24, 2017, 2:00 p.m. – **The Coast Guard has confiscated an abandoned Donzi 38 ZR Competition Speedboat adrift in rough waters a mile and a half east of the Cape Florida Lighthouse off of Key Biscayne.** The search for possible survivors will resume at daybreak, weather permitting. Authorities are working to determine if the speedboat is in any way connected to the recent terrorist activities in Key West. A Glock-18 semi-automatic pistol, cell phone, and laptop were recovered from the boat's rear storage compartment. The vessel has been towed into port for forensic evaluation.

The Key West Post, September 24, 2017, 3:30 a.m. – **The Key West Police Department arrests three on curfew violations, issues statement, "Stay inside or go to jail!"**

The Islamorada News-Press, September 24, 2017, 6:45 a.m. – **The Monroe County Sheriff's Department is labeling the total evacuation of the Florida Keys, from Boca Chica to Key Largo, "a far-reaching success."** Their spokesman added, "With the exception of a few holdouts, everyone's gone. It's like a ghost town."

All emergency operations have been suspended, and nonessential government personnel were instructed to seek shelter on the mainland. US 1 will be closed in both directions starting at 6:00 p.m. today and will remain closed until the storm passes and the road is clear and safe for travel.

The Key West Post, September 24, 2017, 8:45 a.m. – **Botched robbery draws strong words from the Deputy Chief of Police, Captain Bradley Snell.** "They're just a gang of stupid Spics." That was the description Captain Snell gave of the three Cuban-American men after their failed robbery of the Mel Fisher Museum.

After breaking into and starting a fire at the nearby Customs House, ostensibly to create a diversion, the trio used a crowbar to pop the lock on the museum's front door. They were later spotted fleeing on foot with their pockets full of stolen treasure. "They were the only ones on the street, sitting ducks." The captain went on to say, "How stupid is that?" The three men were arrested and are being held at the Monroe County Detention Center on Stock Island.

National Weather Service, Miami, September 24, 2017, 11:00 a.m. – **Hurricane Cindy has weakened slightly after crossing the mountainous region of western Cuba and moving into the Florida Straits.** The storm is headed northwest, with a forward speed of 9 mph, and a barometric pressure of 27.19 MB. With sustained winds of 145 mph, Cindy is expected to make landfall somewhere in the Lower Keys in the early morning hours.

The Key West Post, September 24, 2017, 2:30 p.m. – **Stock Island man drowns attempting to save neighbor's dog.** As the first of Hurricane Cindy's feeder bands slammed the island, Spud, Blanche Montgomery's beloved Basset Hound puppy, managed to escape from her front porch and was washed into the storm drain at the intersection of Cross Street and 7th Avenue. Michael Grey, Blanche's next-door neighbor, witnessed the event and rushed to the dog's rescue. Mr. Grey removed the drain cover, climbed in, and was able to save the dog. Unfortunately, Mr. Grey became trapped and was overcome by the raging water. Attempts to resuscitate Mr. Grey were unsuccessful. He was pronounced dead at the scene.

The Key West Post, September 24, 2017, 6:00 p.m., Kelly Bean reporting – an excerpt: **I caught a ride with Deputy Sally Spence today patrolling the abandoned streets of Key West.** My first reaction, "It's eerie out here." With rain pounding our windshield and wind gusts strong enough to rock the patrol car, we circled the lifeless city. Duval Street, from the Gulf of Mexico to the Atlantic Ocean in three minutes, waves lapping seawalls, the sky a grayish-green, haunting. Houses and businesses boarded up tight, no lights, no revelers. With one hell of a storm on its way, what will tomorrow bring?

I never asked the deputy. I didn't have too. She was as worried as I was. I could see it in her eyes.

The Key West Post, September 25, 2017, 7:30 a.m. – **Key West awakens to devastation.** Hurricane Cindy spared the island of her all-out fury with a last minute jog to the east. One can only imagine how bad things could have been.

High tide coincided with the storm's passing, leaving an estimated forty percent of the island under water. Winds reaching 120 mph toppled trees and power lines, ripped roofs from structures, and wreaked havoc on the island's many mobile homes communities.

Emergency crews are going door-to-door. City crews are working to open roads.

The Lower Keys Medical Center's Emergency Room is overflowing with the injured. "We're seeing mostly cuts and bruises at this point," stated an admissions administrator. No additional casualties have been reported.

The Key West Post, September 26, 2017, 2:00 p.m. – **Residents and business owners' buckle down, yearning for normal.** We all know that things won't seem "normal" again until the lights come on, our toilets flush, and, of course, the tourists return to town. But that isn't stopping the citizens of Key West from getting a head start. Plywood is coming down. People are sweeping water and sand from their living rooms. City crews are seemingly everywhere cleaning out storm pipes, removing rubble, and opening streets. Shipments of ice, food, and water have arrived. FEMA representatives are in town, setting up shop in the Federal Building. And yes, the bars are slowly opening their doors for business.

The Washington Sun, September 28, 2017, 4:30 p.m. – **U.S. Special Operations Forces captured a senior Islamic leader during a raid in eastern Syria, as part of a continuing on-the-ground mission in that country targeting wanted extremists.** Several ISIS militants were killed in the raid and what has been described as a cache of sensitive intelligence documents has been seized.

The operation was conducted at Al-Amr, in the eastern region of Syria, to capture Ali Anjmi, Pentagon officials said. There is no word as to how Ali Anjmi's whereabouts were uncovered.

The Key West Post, October 1, 2017, 6:30 p.m. – **Deputy Chief of Police, Captain Bradley Snell, resigns.** In a surprise move, the twenty-year veteran has left the Key West Police Department. His departure from Police Headquarters was immediate, and attempts to contact him have been unsuccessful. The captain's next-door neighbor told the *Post* that the Snell family is planning a return to their hometown of Birmingham, Alabama. The Police Department issued a one-sentence statement. "We wish Mr. Snell all the best in his future endeavors."

The Key West Post, October 7, 2017, 6:30 p.m. – **Water, sewer, and electricity restored, bridge work ongoing.** In Key West, water faucets are flowing again, and the electricity is back on, at least intermittently. Health Department officials have issued a boil water mandate for all potable water use until further notice. Keys Energy Services warned of roaming blackouts until all facilities have been restored to full operation. The Department of Transportation hopes to have the southbound span of the Boca Chica Bridge ready for two-way travel by this time next week. Fantasy Fest organizers have announced that the festival will go on as planned with activities commencing on October 20th.

The Key West Post, October 10, 2017, 6:30 p.m. – **Mayor returns to light duty.** Mayor Davis made a brief appearance at City Hall today, three weeks after his open-heart surgery. At a gathering of well-wishers, he bragged, "I feel better than I have in years! I'll be running marathons before you know it." He went on to praise his staff for their "monumental and tireless efforts" during his absence. He singled out, Robert Turner, who had been acting as interim mayor. "He did one hell of a job running this town during a time of crisis. He can fill in for me anytime. Thank you, Robert."

PART SEVEN

It's hard to find the right words to say when you see something so beautiful it takes your breath away.

Lounging Gulf side at the Sunset Tiki Bar, we watched the sun slowly disappear. Melting, melting, melting, and with a flash, gone. Left behind: puffy white clouds darting across a sky of deep blue and bright orange, moored sailboats dancing in the choppy surf, seagulls diving for their dinner, a Gulf breeze gentle and warm, two people following in love.

As the crowd slowly shuffled back to the bar, Sara squeezed my hand and turned my way. "You know, Robert, you're a hero."

There they were again, those hazel eyes and that sweet smile, stealing my breath, leaving me speechless.

Clint Bullard, a local favorite, was on stage well into his first set and his second Corona.

You could roll a bowling ball, all the way down Duval, never hit a soul at all, to the Gulf of Mexico.

I chuckled, "A hero? I'm not so sure about that."

The mayor had returned to City Hall full time, and I was happy to be back to my regular duties. The truth was, I had received a commendation from the City Commission, many letters of appreciation, and much to my chagrin, a phone interview with the Today Show. But I wasn't in the mood to talk about me.

We're all in this thing together. If it's not one thing, it's the weather.

Robbie was spending the night with his Uncle Sean. I had told Robbie my plan. He was so excited, I wondered if he'd get any sleep. I had made dinner reservations at Salute for eight o'clock. A walk on the beach would follow. I had a small box burning a

96

hole in my pocket, not an engagement ring, a promise ring. Robbie had told me about them. Go figure.

It's been a perfect day, in every way, when this town takes a rest.

A grayish cloud moved swiftly across the sky forming the likeness of a heart for a split second before breaking into three and moving on. A heart in the sky? A message? A sign?

"Would you like another drink?" I asked. Sara smiled and shook her head.

I stood up and reached out my hand.

"Where are we going?" She had a little girl look on her face that warmed my heart.

While it's just us here, I bet we share a beer, maybe shed a tear, and laugh the night away.

She stood, and we kissed and then kissed again. We parted, catching our breath. It was a moment I'll never forget. There were no words. The look in her eyes said it all.

I took her hand and turned, pulling her gently along.

"Where *are* we going, Robert?"

I smiled and whispered in her ear, "Let's take a walk. I have a bench I need to show you and someone I'd like to introduce you to."

On nights like this, on nights like this, on a night just like this, we own Key West.

About The Authors

1.

Bill Craig is the best-selling author of more than 60 novels spread across the genres from mystery to pulp to science fiction to Westerns. Bill is best known for his *Marlow Key West* mysteries and his *Mitch Cooper* mysteries. Bill often likes to say that it only took him 34 years to become an overnight success. And when introducing himself, he adds that he kills people for a living, much like the fictional Rick Castle on television.

2.

Shirrel Rhoades is a writer, critic, filmmaker, former college professor, art collector, museum president, and publisher. He is the author of *Four Fingers Four Minute Mysteries*, *The Devil's Hop Yard*, *Trapped in a Bahamian Cave*, *The First Gonzo Journalist*, and *Front Row at the Movies*, among many other titles. Rhoades was a co-founder of the annual Mystery Fest Key West. He also edits the annual *Murder in Key West* anthologies. Rhoades and his wife Diane move between Key West and North Carolina with their two rescued dogs and Conch Republic street cat.

3.

Rusty Hodgson *(A/K/A Rusty the Writer)* is a graduate of Yale University where he majored in English Literature and Creative Writing. After graduating with a Juris Doctor degree from the Boston University School of Law, he practiced law for over twenty years in the Boston area, first as a Public Defender, then with his own firm.

He left the practice of law and moved to Key West, Florida, to pursue his passion to write creative fiction. Rusty is a member of the Key West Writers Guild, the winner of the 2012 Key West Mystery Fest Short Story Contest, and also the recipient of the 2017 Florida Keys Council of the Arts Writing Award. He has published six novels.

4.

David Beckwith is a three-generation native of Greenville, Mississippi, with a BBA and an MBA from Ole Miss. David spent 40 years in the securities business, the first half of his career with Bache & Co. and its successors, the second half with Morgan Stanley.

David started writing the Will and Betsy Black Adventure Series in 2010. After moving to Key West, David was tapped to write a book review column for the Key West Citizen, which he continues to produce on a weekly basis.

5.

Earl Smith writes action-adventure thrillers – often with a paranormal twist. The Cabal Series tells the story of a very powerful female detective and her eclectic adopted family. The John Reynolds Saga is an international espionage series. Smith describes himself as a Wondering Monk and Teller of Tall Tales. His friends call him Chief.

6.

Howard Lowell Osterman collected a few rejection slips from popular magazines before deciding he preferred the steady salary of a staff writing position with a newspaper. That led to other "writing gigs" with magazines and book publishers. "A good living," as Osterman tells it. "But in my spare time I kept cranking out novels and short stories, usually working under pseudonyms to avoid conflicts with employers looking for a pound of flesh." He is the author of the thriller Short Changed and Walter the Weirdo Solves a Murder, among other popular works. He has lived in New York, Chicago, and Daytona.

7.

Barthélemy Banks is the nom de plume of a former supervisor for a publishing company that was secretly backed by the CIA. He spent a number of years in the Bahamas where he rubbed elbows with spies, smugglers, international bankers, and reclusive millionaires. Today, he lives part-time on a remote island, where he finds it safe to write about the clandestine world he knows so well.

8.

Robert Coburn is originally from Norfolk, Virginia. After high school in Norfolk, he spent three years in the US Army as a helicopter crew chief stationed in Berlin, Germany. He returned home to attend college at Richmond Professional Institute (Now VCU) in Richmond, Virginia, where he earned a Bachelor of Science degree in Advertising. He also met his wife in Richmond while a student there.

Coburn has worked at major advertising agencies in New York and Los Angeles. His ads have won top awards both nationally and internationally. He is an instrument rated commercial pilot and plays saxophone. He and his wife now live in Carmel, California.

9.

Hollis George is the one-time editorial director of The New Atlantian Library and senior editor of Absolutely Amazing eBooks. A former journalist, college professor, and museum president, he brings a wealth of knowledge to the books he writes and edits.

A long-time denizen of New York City, he enjoys hanging out in the jazz clubs and coffee houses of Greenwich Village as well as prowling the New York City Public Library. Making his home on Copper Square in the East Village, he's fond of the two-for-one beers at McSorley's Tavern, the nearby Ukraine restaurants, and the sidewalk booksellers on Astor Place. He has a small dog named Buttercup.

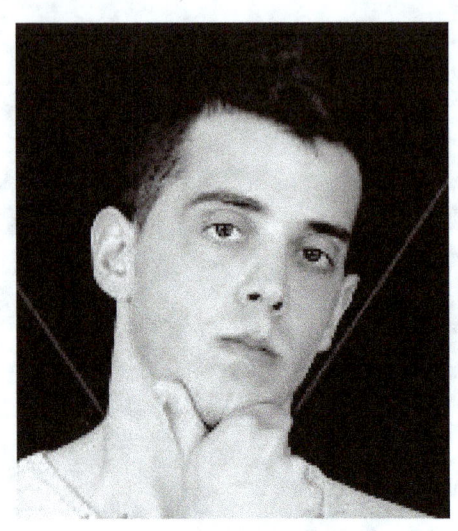

10.

George "Harley" Davidson's unfortunate nickname has carried over from childhood. He has never owned a motorcycle. His first job out of college was in the art department of a daily newspaper, but he gradually moved over to the editorial side. He has worked for publishing houses in New York and London. Sometimes he moves to the other side of the editor's desk to write a book. He has a small dog and loves animals, camping, photography, and road trips in his 1996 van.

11.

Jack Mazur studied creative writing at Southern Connecticut State University in the 1980s under Richard Russo, who would go on to win the Pulitzer for Empire Falls in 2005 or so. Living in Key West, he writes the Jack and Some Palm Trees blog. His friends describe him as a raconteur.

12.

William P. Bahlke is a semi-retired civil engineer pursuing his life-long passion for writing novels. Bill and his wife, Meda, divide their time between the mountains of North Carolina and Key West, Florida. Bill is a graduate of the University of Florida and the author of Frisbee Ball Rules, Popular Demand and Grandpa! Grandpa! What Will I See?

Thank you for reading.
Please review this book. Reviews
help others find Absolutely Amazing eBooks and
inspire us to keep providing these marvelous tales.
If you would like to be put on our email list
to receive updates on new releases,
contests, and promotions, please go to
AbsolutelyAmazingEbooks.com and sign up.

For sales, editorial information, subsidiary rights information
or a catalog, please write or phone or e-mail
AbsolutelyAmazingEbooks
Manhanset House
Shelter Island Hts., New York 11965-0342, US
Tel: 212-427-7139
www.AbsolutelyAmazingEbooks.com
bricktower@aol.com
www.IngramContent.com

For sales in the UK and Europe please contact our distributor,
Gazelle Book Services
White Cross Mills
Lancaster, LA1 4XS, UK
Tel: (01524) 68765 Fax: (01524) 63232
email: jacky@gazellebooks.co.uk